WITHDRAWN

MARINA COHEN

DUNDURN PRESS

TORONTO

Editor: Michael Carroll
Design: Erin Mallory
Printer: Webcom

Library and Archives Canada Cataloguing in Publication

Cohen, Marina
     Ghost ride / by Marina Cohen.

ISBN 978-1-55488-438-4

     I. Title.

PS8605.O378G56 2009   jC813'.6   C2009-903257-0

1 2 3 4 5   13 12 11 10 09

We acknowledge the support of the **Canada Council for the Arts** and the **Ontario Arts Council** for our publishing program. We also acknowledge the financial support of the **Government of Canada** through the **Book Publishing Industry Development Program** and **The Association for the Export of Canadian Books**, and the **Government of Ontario** through the **Ontario Book Publishers Tax Credit** program, and the **Ontario Media Development Corporation**.

Care has been taken to trace the ownership of copyright material used in this book. The author and the publisher welcome any information enabling them to rectify any references or credits in subsequent editions.

J. Kirk Howard, President

Printed and bound in Canada.
www.dundurn.com

Dundurn Press	Gazelle Book Services Limited	Dundurn Press
3 Church Street, Suite 500	White Cross Mills	2250 Military Road
Toronto, Ontario, Canada	High Town, Lancaster, England	Tonawanda, NY
M5E 1M2	LA1 4XS	U.S.A. 14150

Mixed Sources
Product group from well-managed forests, controlled sources and recycled wood or fiber
FSC   www.fsc.org Cert no. SW-COC-002358
© 1996 Forest Stewardship Council

ANCIENT FOREST ™ **FRIENDLY**

For Nonna

ACKNOWLEDGEMENTS

I would like to extend a heartfelt thank-you to the following people: to Dr. David Jenkinson and Martha Martin for their critiques of the manuscript; to my husband, Michael Cohen, for his love and support; to Marsha Skrypuch for her advice and encouragement; to Joni Miyata, Nora and Loic Tuchagues, Anna Marie Crifo, and Grace Wong for cheering me on; and to Sydney, Oscar, and the gang at Castlemore Public School for creating a fabulous book trailer. A very special thank-you to my wonderful agent, Margaret Hart, for believing in this story. And for their expertise, professionalism, and enthusiasm, I would like to thank my editor, Michael Carroll; my publisher, Kirk Howard; and all the people at Dundurn Press.

CHAPTER ONE

Sleepy Hollow. That's what the real-estate agent called it when she dropped off the keys that afternoon. That's what the sign at the crossroads read. An arrow pointed north.

Sam McLean aimed his cellphone straight out the windshield of the Volvo station wagon and clicked. He hit the options key, found the email address he was looking for, and pressed send.

His father frowned. "Put that thing away, Sam. Stop text-messaging and enjoy the ride."

"I wasn't texting. I was sending Mike a picture."

"Of what? The road?"

Sam sighed. "Of the sign. So he'll be able to find me — if he should ever make it out to the butt-of-beyond."

"Watch your language," scolded his father. "Sit up straight and stop slouching."

Sam's thumbs zipped across the keys: *Ill caL U l8r.* "Let you know what life's like in *Creepy Hollow*," he said under his breath.

"What's that?"

"Uh, nothing."

Robert McLean narrowed his eyes. He volleyed glances between the country road and his son in the passenger seat beside him. "You've only had that thing for a week and I'm already regretting buying it." He shook his head. "Remember the deal? Fool with it too much and I'll cut your minutes."

Cut my lifeline, you mean. Sam sighed again and stuffed the phone into the pocket of his jeans. "When are Mom and Miranda getting up here?"

"Just as soon as your mother gives the old house a hundred final checks. You know her. She'll search every corner — make sure we haven't left anything valuable behind, like some dirty dishtowel or old curtain rod." He chuckled.

"I guess," Sam said. But what he wanted to say was: *We did leave something valuable behind — MY LIFE!*

"Hey," Robert said, reading his son's expression. "Ringwood's a nice little town. You'll love it. You'll see."

"I might — if we were actually going to live in Ringwood. But seeing as we're seventy kilometres out of town in the middle of a cow field ..."

"It's seven kilometres, and Sleepy Hollow is hardly a cow field." Robert's voice dropped to lecture tone. "They're huge old homes. You should feel privileged."

Sam rolled his eyes and leaned back against the black leather seat. Privileged. Right. He'd rather be under-privileged and go back to Toronto where he belonged. Where he had Mike. Who was he supposed to hang with here — the cows?

"Start of high school is the perfect time to make a change," his father said.

Sure, thought Sam. *Perfect if you're one of the cool kids. Or a jock. Or goth. Or emo. Or even in the freakin' band. Not so perfect for a nobody.* Thank goodness he'd grown more than twelve centimetres over the summer — at least he wouldn't be the shortest nobody. As the green sign faded into the distance, Sam swallowed a bitter taste.

The station wagon cruised along the Tenth Line, dodging potholes like a snowboarder racing down a mountain of moguls. New housing developments crowded the west side of the two-lane road, while corn-fields sprawled east, broken up now and then by clus-ters of evergreens. Sam caught glimpses of a train that snaked around the trees and farmhouses. "I don't see why we're even moving here," he muttered. "I thought you never wanted to come back."

Robert's grip on the steering wheel tightened for a moment, the skin across his knuckles stretching white before relaxing again. "Things change. People change. Childhood memories fade."

Sam furled his brow. "Huh? What's that supposed to mean?"

His father flashed him a warning. "It means we got a good deal on a great house. The rest is none of your business."

Sam knew when his father had reached his limit, and he knew it was a dangerous line to cross. Besides, what was the point in fighting a done deal?

As the landscape slid past, Sam thought about that name. Sleepy Hollow. Why would anyone name a bunch of houses in the middle of nowhere after some freaky old legend? How did that story go again? Sam wracked his brain. All he could remember was that some dude had lost his head.

His father accelerated as the Volvo proceeded uphill. The sun was low on the horizon, and the twilight filter gave the air a hazy glow.

Sam's mind wandered as details of the old legend came back to him in bits and pieces. He half expected some old-fashioned covered bridge to appear out of nowhere with a headless horseman charging out of it. Thankfully, that didn't happen.

Although what did was almost as strange.

As the car approached the top of the hill, something came at them. Instinctively, Sam dug for his phone, aimed, and clicked. The Volvo swerved to the left and came back too hard, lunging and nearly landing in the ditch as it struggled to correct itself. Everything happened so fast that Sam's brain didn't have time to register details until it was over.

"What the ...?" Sam began, swinging around as much as his seat belt would allow. But even as the words left him the image was taking shape in his mind.

A bike.

A red bike.

Gliding toward them.

Riderless.

CHAPTER TWO

Sam tore at his seat belt and flung open the door as the car skidded to a halt. He raced to the back of the vehicle where the weird-looking bike lay on its side in the middle of the road about thirty metres behind them. Its rear wheel spun slowly. A chilly gust of wind rushed past Sam as he sent the first picture to his email account and snapped off another.

Robert walked toward the bike. He stood with his hands on his hips, scanning the area, a strange expression distorting his face. "Stupid ghost riders." He stopped the wheel with the tip of his shiny black shoe. "They don't think of consequences."

Sam sent the second picture to his email account and clicked a third time.

"I thought I told you to put that thing away!"

After firing off the last picture, Sam tucked the phone out of sight. Then he joined his father by the bike. "Did you say *ghost rider*? As in the comic book?"

Robert scowled and waved a hand dismissively. He

was still searching the roadside for the culprit. "Grab the bike, Sam. Move it to the side before someone crashes into it."

Sam picked up the bike. It had huge wheels and fenders, straight handlebars, and a contraption on the back like a giant mousetrap. The word *Kronan* was written on the crossbar. *This is so retro,* he thought.

A piece of nylon string was tied to one end of the handlebars. It was wrapped around the seat post several times and was attached to the other end of the handlebars, forming a perfect V. Someone had stabilized the wheel so that the bike would go as far as it could before keeling over.

Why would anyone want to do that? Sam wondered as he carried the bike toward the shoulder of the road. He inspected the hilltop and surrounding trees. Not a soul in sight.

"Let's go!" Robert called.

Sam hustled toward the passenger side. Before he shut the door, he couldn't resist a last glance at the ditch that divided the road and fields.

Nothing.

Robert put his key in the ignition and shifted into drive. The Volvo began to roll. "Close call. Dumb kids."

As they picked up speed and got to the top of the hill, Sam gazed out the side window. A flash of bright red near one of the tree trunks snatched his attention. He did a double take, but before he could focus on whatever it was, the Volvo was descending the other side of the hill and the bobbing red blotch had disappeared from view.

Robert shook his head. "Listen, Sam, just watch who you make friends with, okay? It's all about choices. I'm counting on you to make good ones."

Sam nodded. But the way he saw it there were never any choices to be made. His father made them all for him.

The Volvo left the housing development behind as fields stretched out on either side of the road.

"What did you mean by *ghost rider*, Dad?"

Robert looked at his son, then returned his attention to the road. "It's a term for that kind of prank. You know — riding your bike hard and then jumping off and sending it down a hill without you." His thumbs tapped nervously on the steering wheel. "Old stunt. Was even done way back when I was a kid."

Sam arched his eyebrows. His father was the most uptight guy in the world. Never did a single thing wrong. Was this a crack in his shining armour?

"*You* did crazy stuff like that?" Sam asked, sitting a little straighter.

"Who? *Me?*" His father's voice rose as though Sam had asked the most ridiculous question in the world. "Not a chance. I'm not that stupid."

Yeah. Right. Course you aren't. Sam sank into a slouch. He was mad at himself for even entertaining the idea that his father had ever done anything remotely fun.

"Other guys tried it, though," continued his father. "Most without, let's just say, great success."

Sam was interested again. "Yeah? What happened to 'em?"

Robert inhaled deeply. "Major gashes. A few broken bones. Lots of trashed bikes ... among other things ..."

Sam eyed his father. Something was wrong. He wasn't used to hearing a nervous twinge in his father's voice. Was he holding something back? Was he more familiar with *ghost riding* than he was letting on? He studied his father's profile. *Nah. Not him. Not Mr. Perfect.*

The road dipped, and the open field ended abruptly in a forest on the left side. Near a tight huddle of trees the car slowed, and Robert punched the turn signal. The dusty lane they turned into was no bigger than a private driveway. It would have been completely hidden beneath overhanging branches were it not for two enormous stone walls spreading like doors at its entrance. Faded fancy lettering announced: WELCOME TO SLEEPY HOLLOW. On the right Sam noticed a small yellow sign. It read: NO EXIT.

CHAPTER THREE

Sam felt as though he were entering the mouth of a cave. The hanging branches of massive willows, oaks, and cedars blocked all remaining sunlight. The interior lights of the Volvo brightened automatically.

As they entered the hollow, another set of headlights charged toward them, forcing Robert to yank hard on the steering wheel. The Volvo hugged the treeline just as an old blue Ford Mustang blew past.

What is with this place? thought Sam, but his reverie was interrupted by what he spied ahead.

About thirty metres from the main road, the small lane ballooned into a huge circular dead end. Seven houses lined the perimeter, each one larger and creepier than the previous. Fieldstone foundations, dark brick or faded vertical siding, looming octagonal turrets, and wide wraparound verandahs — they were all hideously magnificent.

Sam's eyes fixed on number four. A moving van was parked in front of it. The house was a two-and-a-half-storey monster with a complex series of roofs and a variety of windows. It looked at least a hundred years old. Part of it was covered in some kind of creeping vine. A worn basketball hoop with a ragged net hung from the detached garage set slightly back from the house.

"So what do you think?" Sam's father asked.

Everyone in the family had already seen the house except for Sam. He had refused to go. It had been his way of protesting the move.

"*This* is our new house?" Sam's tone was a mixture of apprehension and awe.

His father grinned proudly "I told you you'd like it here."

Sam scanned the surroundings. The old homes and huge properties had to be worth a fortune. "Uh, Dad," he began cautiously, "I know it's not my business, but ..."

Robert finished his son's question. "How can we afford it?"

Sam raised his eyebrows and nodded.

Robert opened the car door. The musky scent of country air seeped inside. He stepped onto the driveway and stared at the house. "It's a funny thing. Growing up in the shabby bungalows in town, I'd known about these houses —" Sam's father seemed suddenly thoughtful, almost sad "— but I never thought I'd ever be able to own one."

Stepping out of the car, Sam moved slowly toward the house. "Uh, Dad, that didn't exactly answer my question."

"It's not complicated. Housing prices in Toronto have gone crazy. The land alone is worth a fortune in today's market. Throw in a vendor desperate for a quick sale, and believe it or not, we pretty much traded even-steven."

"You're kidding." Sam thought about his house in Toronto. It was a bug compared to this beast.

Robert smiled. "You just need to be willing to fix up a place. And be willing to move out to the *butt-of-beyond*."

Sam couldn't believe it. His father had actually said the word *butt*. There was a first time for everything.

Three men got out of the van and approached Sam's father. While they discussed the logistics of the move, Sam's mother's car pulled into the driveway. Miranda sprang out before the vehicle came to a complete stop.

"It's great, isn't it?" she cried, rushing up to Sam. "Did you check out the backyard? It's huge and it has a ravine that leads down to a creek!"

"We just got here, *Moronda*," Sam said. "How could I have time to see all that?"

Miranda slapped him on the shoulder and whined, *"Mommm!"*

"Don't call your sister names, Sam," his mother said. She reached into her car and pulled out a box. "Why don't you take a look around the neighbourhood? Let the movers get the large furniture into the house. You can start to unpack later. It's going to be a long night."

Sam peered into the gloom. *Neighbourhood? Is that what you call seven houses stuck in the middle of nowhere?*

"Why not?" he mumbled. "It's not like we can get lost or anything."

Sam was about to head around the back of the house when his eyes were drawn to the topmost window. For a second he thought he saw a dark figure standing there. Then he blinked, and the shadow was gone.

CHAPTER FOUR

At a quarter past ten in the evening Sam was unpacking his clothes and personal junk when he heard the doorbell chimes echo through the hallway and all the way up to the third floor. He flew down two flights of creaky stairs to check it out.

Miranda was already at the entrance with Sam's mother only a few steps behind. Sam hung back. He sat on the steps, watching his sister swing open the heavy wooden door.

A woman and a guy about the same age as Sam stood on the porch. The woman was short and thin with frizzy black hair. She wore a black wool shawl around her shoulders. In her hands she clutched a casserole dish. The guy had the same frizzy hair. He stared at his feet as if he didn't want to be there.

"Can I help you?" Sam's mother asked, joining Miranda.

"Oh … yes … uh, hello. I'm your neighbour. Number five. I just wanted to welcome you to Sleepy Hollow. I thought you … well, I wondered if … perhaps you might not have eaten … yet." She held out the casserole dish.

In the hall light Sam could see it contained lasagna. He frowned. *What kind of idiot brings someone lasagna at ten o' clock at night?*

Sam's mother smiled warmly. "Thank you. How thoughtful." She accepted the dish. "It looks delicious. Why don't you come in?" She motioned for the pair to enter.

The woman shook her head. "No, it's late. I'm sure you're busy getting settled. We just wanted to welcome you."

Sam's mother gave the dish to Miranda and held out her hand. "You must have some sort of sixth sense because we haven't eaten." The two women shook hands. "I'm Elizabeth McLean. And this is my daughter, Miranda." She stepped back and pointed at Sam. "That's my son, Sam."

"My name's Maeve Moon. And this is Walter."

Wally Moon? Sam covered his mouth to conceal his grin.

The guy glanced up briefly and locked eyes with Sam. He pushed his huge black-framed glasses higher on the bridge of his nose, forced a smile, then looked at his feet again. His pants were two inches too short and twenty years out of style. His sweater had to be homemade.

"Walter's starting the ninth grade," Maeve said. "The real-estate agent mentioned something about your son being around the same age."

Sam's stomach lurched. It was suddenly clear where this was headed. It was a setup. They had let a Trojan horse into their house. Sam cleared his throat to get his mother's attention, but it was too late.

"Sam starts Ringwood District High School on Tuesday, too. He'll be on the same bus as Walter. They can ride together, right, Sam?"

Un-freakin'-believable!

Sam had a vision of himself heading into the halls of his new high school with good ol' Wally stuck to him like gum on his shoe. He might as well be wearing a huge neon sign around his neck that screamed: *I'm a geek!*

He heard a click in his brain. The vault he kept there was opening. He willed it shut. He wasn't going back there. Not now. Not ever.

Although Sam mumbled, "Uh, sure," his expression said, *No way!*

"Good," Maeve said, completely oblivious to the look of horror plastered across Sam's face. She took a deep breath, then added another "Good."

"Are you sure you don't want to come inside?" Elizabeth asked.

"No. We'll be going now. But I'm sure we'll see a great deal of each other. Small neighbourhood, isn't it?"

Maeve nudged her son. He forced another smile, then they both turned to leave.

As soon as the deadbolt clicked, Sam turned to his mother. "I don't believe you! How could you do that to me? Why'd you go and promise I'd hang with that guy? Are you trying to ruin any chance I have of making real friends around here?"

"You watch your tone with me," his mother said, "or I can think of a few privileges that'll disappear quickly — starting with your computer, your iPod, and your phone."

Sam gritted his teeth and glared at his mother.

"What's all this about?" Sam's father asked, joining the group. He was wearing a heavy sweatshirt. His arms were crossed around his chest. "Who was that? What did they want?"

To ambush me, thought Sam, but he knew better than to say anything out loud in front of his father. He kept his mouth shut and continued to scowl.

"Our new neighbours," Elizabeth said. "Our *nice* new neighbours." She met Sam's gaze head-on. "They dropped by to give us a dish of lasagna."

Robert grinned. "Lasagna? That's great. I'm starving." He took the casserole from Miranda. "Who are they?"

"Number five," Miranda said. "Maeve and Walter."
She wrinkled her nose.

"Last name is Moon," Elizabeth said.

"Did you say *Moon*?" Robert's voice had faded to a
whisper.

"As in lunar body," Elizabeth said. "Sound familiar?"

Robert's brow furled as though he were thinking
really hard about something. "No," he said finally, shaking his head. "I don't think so."

Sam's father blinked several times and then began to
sway. His arms drooped, and the lasagna dish nearly fell
from his grasp. He steadied himself against the wall with
his shoulder and shivered.

"Are you okay, Daddy?" Miranda asked.

"You don't look well," Elizabeth said.

"I think I'm coming down with the flu. Turn on the
heat. This house is freezing."

CHAPTER FIVE

Miranda flew through the hall. "Hurry up! Or we'll miss the bus!"

Pulling on his grey hoodie, Sam slung his backpack over one shoulder, grabbed an apple from the bowl of fruit on the kitchen table, and trailed after her.

"Enjoy your first day!" his mom called.

"Make good choices," he heard his dad say as he pulled the door shut behind him.

"*Riiiight* ..." he muttered to himself. *They already made my first choice for me — my new best friend, Wally.* He winced at the thought.

Light forced its way through the thick and intertwining branches, speckling the ground so that even in the morning light, Sleepy Hollow appeared sleepy. Sam stood on the porch and checked the neighbourhood, then exhaled.

Walter was nowhere to be seen.

Sam had spent most of the Labour Day long weekend unpacking, arranging things in his room, and worrying about how he'd get out of hanging with Walter.

Maybe the guy would get sick and miss the first day of school. Maybe *really* sick and miss the whole first week. The first semester? Nah. That was too much to hope for. Besides, Sam didn't wish any real harm on the guy. He just didn't want to be stuck with him. Maybe Walter could miss the bus. That would be enough to buy Sam some time.

He sucked in a lungful of crisp autumn air. Although it was technically still summer, he could taste fall at the back of his throat.

Sam studied the semi-circle of houses. The blue Mustang was parked on the street in front of number seven. An old lady was sitting in a rocking chair on the verandah at number two. No sign of life at number five. He hustled toward the main road.

Miranda was already in the straightaway. "Come on, Sam! You're gonna be late!"

"Coming, *Moronda*!"

Miranda glared at him, shook her head disdainfully, and pulled her pink school case behind her, strutting like a miniature flight attendant.

Sam grinned. He loved teasing his sister. She was an easy target — just as uptight and anal as his father.

When he broke through the shelter of trees, the bright sunlight forced him to squint. Through half-closed eyes he spied two figures standing by the side of the road and stopped short. Beside Miranda was Walter — frizzy hair, geeky pants, ugly cardigan, and all.

Sam only had a few seconds to think. He dug into his pocket, yanked out his iPod, and jammed the plugs into his ears. Strolling to the edge of the road, he stood there, calm and cool, in his own little world. After he took a huge bite of his apple, he hit the play button on the iPod and was assaulted by a cascade of violins. Nearly choking on his apple, he coughed, swallowed, coughed again, then hit the skip button.

Mr. Perfect strikes again!

When Sam got the iPod for his fourteenth birthday, it came with two conditions. One: his father had to approve every single song he downloaded. No foul language. No violence, et cetera, et cetera. Two, and far worse: every second song had to be *classical!* Beethoven, Tchaikovsky, Chopin, Vivaldi, for crying out loud! It was a stupid idea. As if *he*, Sam, was going to listen to classical music. He just hit the skip button, and that was that. *Ba-bye, Bach. S'long, Stravinsky. Adiós, Amadeus.*

Much better, he thought as gut-thudding bass shook the fillings in his teeth. While he bobbed his chin to the relentless beat, he noticed Walter glance at him, then look away.

Come on, bus. Hurry up! Sam leaned into the road. No sign of the rolling yellow deathtrap. Not yet.

He took another bite of the apple and risked a sideways peek. Walter was shifting nervously. Was he getting ready to make a move? Sam closed his eyes and willed the bus, wherever it was, to hit the gas. When Sam opened his eyes, he nearly fell over. Miranda was right in his face.

"What are you listening to?" she demanded.

Sam saw Walter's eyes drift toward the conversation. *"Whaaat?"* He pretended he couldn't hear his sister.

She tried again. "What … are … you … listening … to?"

"Huhhh?" He tapped his ears in an exaggerated gesture as though he couldn't hear a thing.

Walter was on the move. It was a chilly autumn morning, but Sam still felt ice-cold. His fingertips prickled. He wanted to shove his sister away. She was ruining everything.

"I know you can hear me, Sam. What's your problem?"

"Stop bugging me!" he snapped, pushing her shoulder and nearly knocking her down.

Walter was only a few feet away. Sam swung around and started to walk off, pitching the rest of his apple into the sky. It sailed up, arched downward, and smashed into bits in the middle of the road. Just then he saw a yellow-orange blur appear on the horizon.

Perfect timing. Now I just need to let Walter get on the bus first.

"I'm telling on you, Sam!" Miranda cried. "You're gonna be in big trouble. Mom's gonna take your iPod away for sure."

Probably, he thought, *but it won't matter then, will it?*

The bus screeched to a halt, and the door opened. Miranda stomped toward the vehicle and got on.

That left Walter.

He's got to get on first, otherwise he might follow me. Sam dropped to one knee and began retying an already-fastened shoelace.

The bus driver honked. When Sam looked up, he was alone on the side of the road. A cold wind tousled his sandy brown hair, yet he felt warmer than he had a moment earlier.

When Sam got on the bus, it was a hive of activity. Miranda sat in the front seat beside a girl with red hair and freckles. His sister scowled at him as he walked by. Walter was sitting alone midway, watching Sam through thick-rimmed glasses. Sam passed his new neighbour without comment. Although he felt a twinge of guilt, he shook it off as he shuffled to the back of the bus and plunked himself into a free seat in the last row.

Sam turned up the volume on his iPod. One of his favourite rap songs boomed in his ears. The bus bounced south along the Tenth Line toward town, passing the spot where the riderless bike had come to its final stop in the middle of the road. He scanned the brush. No sign of anything bright red bobbing there now.

The bus halted twice in the new housing development, and several kids of various ages, each dressed in the latest trends, cellphones, and MP3 players, boarded. Everyone went by Walter as though he wasn't there.

Man, that guy's like people repellent, Sam thought.

At the crossroads the bus turned onto Main Street and headed into town. For the first time Sam got a glimpse of Ringwood — and apparently that was all he needed. A gas station, a grocery store, a post office, and a library slid past his window. He turned in time to see a shabby restaurant called the Lion and the Lamb, some kind of municipal building, and a police station fly by on the other side of the road. Back out his own window, he saw a variety store, a dance studio, and a used-clothing boutique flash by. Ringwood. That was it. Good thing he hadn't blinked or he would have missed everything.

Sam had just settled back, hitting the skip button to avoid the hauntingly repetitive music of Ravel's Boléro, when the bus squealed to a crawl, took a hard right, and swung into a side street. Rows of tiny bungalows with sagging roofs and junk-filled yards lined the street. A metal shopping cart and a busted trash can littered the sidewalk. This was where his father had grown up.

The bus door opened, and another crowd of kids got on. These definitely seemed tougher than those living in the new housing development. Two guys pushed their way to the rear. One threw himself into the empty seats in front of Sam, while the other hopped into the row beside him. The guy beside Sam wore a black hoodie and baggy pants; the guy in front sported a bright red Buffalo Bills toque. That shade of red was hard to forget — Sam recognized it immediately as the bobbing red blur that had been hiding in the trees when the riderless bike had come at them.

A girl was making her way down the aisle, as well. She was tall and thin with stringy blond hair. She had been contemplating the floor, but before she sat in the empty row beside the guy in the red toque, she caught Sam staring at her.

CHAPTER SIX

The bus came to a grinding stop in front of Ringwood Middle School. The younger kids left the vehicle in a frenzy. Sam shook his head and rolled his eyes. *You'd think the school's handing out free candy.*

Miranda was one of the first to exit. Sam peered out the window and watched her drag her school case along the sidewalk, heading toward the yard. He could tell she was still angry at him. Under normal circumstances she probably would have glanced back and smiled. Maybe even waved. Today he was lucky she didn't throw a rock at him.

"Whatcha listening to?" asked the guy slumped in the row in front of Sam. Beneath the bright red toque his eyes were hooded. He took up the entire row, his long legs splayed into the aisle. Somehow he didn't strike Sam as the type to ride a Kronan bike.

Before Sam could prevent him, the guy reached over. He snatched Sam's iPod and plugged it into his ears.

"Hey!" Sam protested, but the guy smacked his hand away.

Red Toque burst out laughing. "Yo, J-Man! Check this out!" He threw the iPod to his friend in the row beside Sam. The guy had a quick listen and began cackling.

Sam's stomach bottomed out. The song must have changed. The girl, who had been chatting with Red Toque and Black Hoodie, now gazed directly at Sam. Their eyes locked a second time. Could she see the panic in them? Sam blinked and looked away.

"Classical music?" Black Hoodie wailed. "What a wonk!" His laughter sounded like a wounded hyena's. "What a scrub!"

Other kids turned to stare at Sam. Suddenly, he felt as if he were on display in a zoo.

This can't be happening. Sam's eyes found the back of Walter's head. In the same instant Walter glanced back. His face was pale, expressionless.

"Come on, guys, give it back to him," the blond girl said.

Red Toque's smile faded. *"Come on, guys, give it back to him,"* he mocked. "What's he to you, AJ? Your new best friend?"

Sam's cheeks burned. He realized that Red Toque and AJ were together and that Red Toque wasn't impressed with her sticking up for Sam. Besides, he couldn't let himself be defended by a girl. He lunged over and yanked back his iPod from a still-laughing J-Man, but it didn't matter. The damage was done.

Red Toque chuckled again and shook his head. "Yo, dude, whatcha listening to that junk for?"

"I *don't* listen to it." Sam stuffed his iPod into his pocket.

"Yeah, right. Someone must have snatched your Pod and swapped tunes. Some *ghost*, maybe?" He snapped his fingers at J-Man, and they both exploded in laughter as if it were the funniest thing they'd ever heard.

This was bad. Sam remembered what Mike had taught him. Mike had said you could cruise through high school on nothing but reputation. Now Sam's reputation had sprung a leak, and he was sinking fast. He had to do something and quick. Before he knew what was happening, he squared his shoulders to Red Toque and fixed him with hard eyes. "Quit baggin' on me, man." That was exactly what Mike would have said.

Red Toque's spine straightened. Obviously, he wasn't used to people standing up to him. His eyes grew wide. He studied Sam, looking him up and down with a mixture of curiosity and contempt. Then he settled back into his seat and grinned. "What's your name?"

"What's yours?" The cool-guy act was working. Sam had to keep it up. These were the guys he had to win over. He had to gain their respect.

"Don't be all salty with me," Red Toque said. "Maniac's the name. Thrill-seeking's the game."

AJ rolled her eyes.

Sam frowned. "Thrill-seeking?"

Maniac snorted. "This kid belongs in kindergarten. Needs to learn his ABCs."

J-Man reached over and gave Maniac some exploding knuckles, and the two began laughing all over again. "Send him to your blog, Maniac. It'll teach him what thrill-seeking is pretty quick."

Great, thought Sam, rolling his eyes, *back to square one*. He sank hopelessly into his seat while the two continued their taunts.

Maniac smirked. "*Awww!* He's lost without his Beethoven. I think he's gonna cry!"

More laughter.

"What'd he say his name was?" J-Man asked.

"He didn't," Maniac said.

"How about we give him a name then? How about we call him *Maestro*!"

"Yeah, I like that. Hey, Maestro, my grandma says she wants to borrow your Pod. Says you two got the same taste in music."

Perfect, thought Sam, *just what I've always wanted — a nickname*.

He decided to ignore them. Someone who called

themselves Maniac was either an idiot or a psycho — and there was no telling what either was capable of. Sam was pretty sure he'd already witnessed some of Maniac's so-called thrill-seeking — the stunt with the red bike that could have easily cost him and his father their lives if another vehicle had been approaching.

Sam took a deep breath and exhaled slowly. At least these guys, unlike Walter, were cool. Given the choice he'd take psycho over geek any day.

The bus pulled into the loop of Ringwood Secondary. The older kids exited, dragging their feet as though they were dead men walking. Part of Sam was thinking he should get up and push his way through the crowd, try to get away from the two guys as quickly as possible. The other part of him said he should stay put.

Relax, show no fear, Mike always said.

AJ stood and began making her way up the aisle.

"Let's bounce, Javon," Maniac said.

"Yo, Cody, grab my backpack," AJ said, swinging around and motioning to the seat where she'd left it.

Cody and Javon.

It was as if someone had thrown a switch. Suddenly, these guys seemed a lot less threatening. Sam took a deep breath and steadied his nerves. He remained seated as the two guys shuffled up the aisle. AJ had gotten off the bus, and so had Javon. Just then Sam got an idea. "Yo, *Cody.*"

The guy halted and swung round.

This was Sam's only chance. He couldn't blow it. "My dad drives a black Volvo. Ring a bell?"

Cody narrowed his eyes as Sam rose and started walking toward him. "You've got a blog, right? I think I have some pictures you might be interested in."

Sam dangled his cellphone like bait on a hook.

CHAPTER SEVEN

The air in Sleepy Hollow smelled like a closet full of last season's clothes. Each time he inhaled, Sam swore he tasted mothballs.

As he sauntered from the Tenth Line through the tunnel of branches, Sam had to practically dive to avoid the blue Mustang that thundered down the street. He spun round and watched the vehicle barrel onto the main road without even pretending to slow down, let alone come to a full stop.

"How was your first day?" his mother asked when he entered the house. "Classes go all right?"

"Okay, I guess," Sam said, even though the day had ended up being pretty darn good.

For one thing, Walter wasn't in any of his classes — not one. And apparently Walter had missed the bus back home. *Too bad*, thought Sam, grinning. But best of all, Sam had managed to hold his own with Maniac. It was the first step in getting the guy to accept him.

Sam yanked the heavy wooden door, slamming it

accidentally. The entire house shook.

"Keep it down," his mother said, stepping into the foyer. "Your father's not feeling well. He worked from home today. He's upstairs having a nap right now."

Sick? I can't remember the last time Mr. Perfect missed a day at the office, thought Sam. *Not like he ever lets me take a day off school ...*

Dropping his backpack in the hall, Sam moved toward the stairs. "Did the cable guy come? Is the wireless hooked up?" He couldn't wait to check out Cody's blog, not to mention access his email account and send Cody the pictures that would solidify their friendship.

"Wireless is up and running." His mother turned and headed toward the kitchen. "Shame you won't be able to use it until *tomorrow*," she added casually over her shoulder.

Sam stopped short. Miranda stood at the top of the stairs, arms folded, grinning ear to ear. She fanned her fingers mockingly.

"You're such a rat, *Moronda*," Sam snarled. "A skinny, slimy *rat*!"

"*Moooommmm!* Sam's calling me names again!"

"Two days," his father said, appearing behind Miranda.

Robert had a woollen blanket wrapped around his shoulders. His eyes looked as if he hadn't slept in days.

The calmness in his voice was a warning. It said: *Don't push it.* He'd taken away Sam's computer privileges for an entire month once and hadn't even batted an eye.

Sam frowned, choking back his anger. He muscled past Miranda, marched up the second flight of stairs to his room, and threw himself onto his bed.

Sam's new room was the third-floor loft. It was fairly large, housing his bed, a nightstand, a dresser, and a desk. On the walls Sam had pinned a few posters — two of his favourite rap singers and one of a girl in a bikini and high heels, leaning over a red Porsche. After only four days, the hardwood floor was already littered with socks, boxers, jeans, and T-shirts so that the blue area rug was lost beneath the various piles of washed and unwashed laundry. If his father saw the mess, he'd be all over him. He liked having the third floor to himself.

Sam dug his cell out of his jeans. He searched his list, scrolled to Mike's number, and pressed talk.

"Hey," said the familiar voice of his best friend.

"Hey."

"What's doing up there?"

"Not much," Sam said. "You?"

"Same old."

"How was your first day? Who's all in your classes?"

"Ryan's in English and math with me. Harjot's with me in science and art."

Sam chuckled. "You took *art*?"

"Yeah? So? I needed something easy."

"You can't draw worth crap." Sam could feel the anger in him settle like fizz on a freshly poured can of pop. He missed Mike. He'd never say it, of course, but then again he didn't have to. "So are your parents gonna let you come up here some time?"

"Probably, but not for a while. You're practically in a different time zone, you know."

Sam sighed. "Yeah. Maybe next month or something?"

"Sure."

They talked for a while about school, teachers, sports, and girls. Sam was about to tell Mike all about Maniac, Javon, and AJ when he heard his mom calling him. "Gotta go."

"Easy."

Sam stared at his phone for a moment and then pressed end.

"Coming," he said when his mother shouted a second time. Sam trudged down the stairs and into the kitchen where his mother was preparing dinner.

When she saw him, she wiped her hands on a dishtowel and reached for the clean lasagna dish that had been sitting on the counter for the past couple of days. "Will you take this over to Walter's house for me?"

Sam rolled his eyes. "*Me*? Do I *have* to?"

"Yes." She handed him the dish.

"Why can't you do it? Or Miranda?" He could see his sister making faces at him from the family room.

"Because I asked *you*."

Sam eyed the dish as though it were a giant wad of used tissues.

"Listen, take the dish over to Ms. Moon and I'll talk to your father. Maybe I can get him to knock off a day from your Internet sentence."

He snatched the dish. "Fine. I'll drop it off, but it's not like I'm gonna go over and hang out with that guy or anything ..." But even as the words left him, Sam got an idea. Maybe ol' number five could be some use to him, after all.

Sam cut across his lawn and up Walter's driveway. He studied the house as he approached. There was something odd about it. Sam couldn't quite put his finger on what it was, but somehow the place gave him the creeps. Not that any of the old houses in Sleepy Hollow appeared particularly inviting, but this one seemed somehow ... different.

He held the glass dish under one arm as he walked up the steps to the porch. The paint on the front door was cracked and faded. The windows were grungy. The drapes were drawn so that Sam couldn't tell if there were any lights on in the house. He reached up and hammered the rusty knocker twice. The sound was thick and dull. He took a step backward.

Seconds passed. No answer.

Something prickled the back of Sam's neck, and beneath his sweatshirt the fine hair on his arms stood on end. He had the distinct feeling he was being watched.

Carefully, he peered over his shoulder and searched the area. The street was empty except for the old lady sitting in her rocker at number two. She faced his direction, rocking back and forth. Was it *her* eyes crawling under his skin?

He considered her for a few seconds. Other than the slow rocking the woman sat completely still as if someone had placed a mannequin in the chair and was moving it by remote control.

When Sam turned toward the door again, the breath caught in his throat. He sprang back and nearly tumbled down the steps, grabbing the handrail at the last second and steadying himself. Luckily, he managed to hang on to the dish.

Walter was standing right in front of him.

"Crap!" Sam said, finding his balance. "You nearly gave me a heart attack."

Walter merely stared.

"Don't you know better than to go sneaking up

on someone?" Sam practically shoved the dish into the guy's gut. "Here!"

Walter took the dish mechanically. He looked down at it as though there was something amusing about it. Sam scowled, shook his head, and started to leave.

"You're the one who came here," Walter said. His voice was small, almost a whisper.

Sam swung around. "What?"

"I said *you're* the one who came *here*."

"So? What's that got to do with anything?"

"How can *I* sneak up on *you* when *you* came *here*."

Walter had a point. Sam frowned. A strange glint in the boy's eyes made Sam even angrier.

"Look, dude ..." Sam waved a hand dismissively. He took a few steps toward his house, calling over his shoulder, "I just came by to return that dish. That's all. And —" Sam could see the old woman still rocking back and forth in her chair. "And ..." He knew he was going to hate himself. "And to see if maybe you had Internet access ..."

He waited. The rocking chair was mesmerizing. *Back and forth. Back and forth.*

Walter didn't respond.

Sam tried again as he turned to face Walter "I *said* ..." The rest of his sentence died in his throat. He swallowed. The porch was empty. Walter was gone.

CHAPTER EIGHT

Sam stomped back into his house and marched into the kitchen.

"So?" his mother asked. It was a simple word, but it was loaded.

"What?" Sam threw open a cupboard and rifled through it for a snack.

"Did you give the dish back?"

"Yeah." He grabbed a handful of chocolate chip cookies and popped two into his mouth whole.

His mother paused. She eyed Sam in that unique way that always made him feel guilty even when he hadn't done anything wrong.

"What?" he asked, sputtering crumbs.

"Dinner will be ready in five minutes." She took the rest of the cookies from his hand and was about to turn when she added, "You know, you could give the poor guy a chance."

Sam practically choked "Poor guy? Who? Walter? A chance to do what?"

Now more than ever, Sam disliked Walter. For one thing, Wally had scared the crap out of him. Then the kid had had the nerve to leave without even saying a word. This guy wasn't only a loser; it was as if he didn't even *care* that he was.

"To be friends," Elizabeth said.

Sam rolled his eyes and sighed. "*Friends?* I already told you, Mom. I'm not going to be friends with him." Sam felt he needed to spell things out for his mother once and for all, or she wouldn't stop bugging him. "First of all, he's a geek. *A total geek.* He dresses all geeky like he's only got one set of clothes. And second, he creeps me out. He's always staring at me funny and stuff."

Elizabeth moved closer to her son, and her voice dropped to a whisper. "I can remember a time, not so long ago, that *you* didn't have many friends."

Sam quit chewing and shot her a venomous look. It was as if she'd drawn back a bow, waited for the right moment, and then let the arrow fly straight into his heart.

But Sam's mother wasn't done. She let loose with a second arrow. "Don't you remember what that was like?"

Remember? No, he didn't remember. He didn't want to remember. He'd managed to cram all those memories into a huge metal box, bolt it shut, and shove it far into the recesses of his mind where even he couldn't find it. He'd forgotten all about what it was like to be the kid no one wanted to play with. No one wanted to sit beside. No one wanted to talk to. Those days were gone for good.

Everything had changed the day Mike had come into his life. Mike had moved into the house next door when the two of them were in grade six and had befriended Sam. With Mike's help, Sam had reinvented himself.

No, Sam wasn't going to relive the awful days before Mike. Not for anything or anyone. Least of all for Walter.

"All I'm saying is," his mother continued, "would it kill you to show a little kindness?"

Sam frowned, took a deep breath, and exhaled through flaring nostrils. "Kill me? No. Try obliterate me."

Just then his father entered the kitchen, still wrapped in a wool blanket. "Don't you have homework to do, Sam?"

This is great. Mom wants to make me a geek. Dad wants to mould me into his own perfect image. Can't they both just leave me alone?

————————

Sam awoke with a start. Sweat trickled down his forehead. His heart hammered against his rib cage.

He must have had a nightmare, but the moment he'd opened his eyes, it was snuffed out. He lay there catching his breath, trying to recall what it was that could have scared him half to death. All he could remember was the colour red. Somehow the dream had been red.

Outside, rain battered his window. The illuminated digits on his alarm clock read 1:09 a.m. Sam shut his eyes. Taking a few deep breaths, he sat up, swung his legs over the side of the bed, and ran his fingers through his scraggly hair. The fear that was now fading behind a curtain of fog in his brain was replaced with anger.

Sam had never been completely disobedient before, but this time his father was asking for it. He didn't deserve to lose his computer privileges for calling his sister a few harmless names. After all, it wasn't as if she hadn't had it coming.

Walking over to his desk, Sam switched on his laptop. While he waited for it to boot up, he searched the piles of clothes on the floor for the jeans he'd worn the previous day. His pulse was steady now. The incessant drumming of the rain was soothing.

What had he been dreaming about? Why was his memory drenched in red?

He found his jeans and dug into the pocket, pulling out the crumpled piece of paper on which he'd scrawled the name of Cody's blog: *maniacstunts.badblog.com*. Cody's email address would be in the contact section of his profile. *Perfect*, thought Sam, *but first things first*.

Sam crept toward the door and opened it a crack.

He could see down to the lower hallway. It was pitch-black. That was good. Sam slipped through the door and tiptoed across the upper landing. He stood for a moment and listened. Aside from the relentless hammering of rain on the windows and roof, all he could hear was his father's raspy breathing.

Fast asleep. And what he doesn't know won't hurt him.

Sam snuck back to his room and sat at his desk. He launched his Internet provider and held his breath. It opened. He released a sigh of relief. *I'm in!*

His fingers sped across the keyboard, and in seconds Cody's blog popped up on the screen. It was the coolest thing Sam had ever seen. The title, *Maniac Stunts*, had letters dripping with blood. They were emblazoned across a background of skulls and bones that seemed real, not animated. On the right-hand side was an "About Me" section, but instead of a picture of Cody, there was a photo of the head of a Doberman pinscher, its lips curled in a fierce snarl, its fangs fully exposed, foam drooling from the corners of its jaws. Beside the photo it said: "Name: Maniac. Location: Sticksville, Butt of the World."

Sam grinned. *Exactly. This guy gets it.*

The last entry was dated two weeks ago. The title was "What a Ride!"

Check out this dope stunt. It was too hot.
Last Sunday night I rode down Vinegar Hill
on three boards. It was a huge rush! I must
have been doing a hundred. I had no idea
how I was going to stop, but hey, who cares
about that stuff? Check it out!

Posted: August 21, 11:30 p.m.

The photo wasn't clear. The background was dark
and there was a blur in the centre. Sam squinted. He
was pretty sure he could make out the body of Cody,
lying stretched out, almost flat on the ground with three
skateboards under him. His arms were spread like wings.
He looked as if he were flying. Five comments were
posted. Sam clicked on them. The first comment was
from Homegirl:

Yo, Maniac, that was pretty M&M. But it's
been done to *death* ... literally!

Posted: August 21, 11:49 p.m.

The next message was from J-Man:

M&M? *Mediocre?* Yo! Maniac, Homegirl
don't know nothing. That stunt was off the

hook! Especially when that big body came right at you and you had to roll off into the ditch!

Posted: August 22, 12:03 p.m.

There were three more messages. Two approving of Cody, but one that said he was a total moron. The person went on to say they knew a kid who had sliced his leg open clear to the bone doing that exact stunt. Nearly bled to death.

Somehow, thought Sam, *Cody doesn't strike me as the type to worry about minor details like bleeding to death!*

Sam scrolled down. There were several more entries with pictures of bizarre stunts. Cody tobogganing off the roof of a garage. Cody riding a shopping cart down the street. And one Sam couldn't quite figure out: Cody trying to do what appeared to be a back flip in the middle of a parking lot. Sam shook his head. *I'm not sure if this guy is really cool or really stupid.* Either way, Sam was intrigued.

Below the photo of the Doberman was a section entitled "Links to Cool Dudes." The long list included Homegirl, J-Man, and a bunch of other weird names. Sam thought he should check out some of them, but not tonight. This evening he was on a mission.

Thunk!

Sam snapped to attention. What was that noise? His father? If he was caught now, he'd lose his Internet privileges for an entire year. And that wouldn't even be the worst of it.

He sat completely still. Should he shut off his laptop and dive for his bed? He strained his ears.

Thunk!

Sam relaxed. The sound was coming from outside. His desk was right by the window. He leaned over and lifted the heavy curtain. Sam had a clear view of the street. Someone was standing in the driveway beside a red car at number six. Through the darkness and rain Sam couldn't tell if it was a man or a woman. He couldn't see a face, or a head for that matter, since the person was under a large black umbrella. Whoever it was, he or she kept opening and closing the trunk of the car.

This is the creepiest neighbourhood, thought Sam, shaking his head and letting the curtain fall.

He had to be quick. His father just might wake up if the guy continued to make noise.

Sam minimized Cody's blog and opened his email account. He clicked send/receive and waited as some thirty-five messages downloaded. Most were junk mail — advertisements for the latest medications, stock market picks, and people trying to sell him useless stuff. But three emails were as good as gold. They contained the pictures he'd sent himself of the riderless bike. Those photos were his in with Cody.

Minimizing his email account, he returned to Cody's blog, clicked on contact, and watched an email box open with Cody's address. Sam memorized it, went back to his email, and forwarded all three messages with attachments to Cody. He hadn't even looked at the pictures yet, but he was sure they had turned out all right. In the body of the last email he wrote: "Cool stunt. Lucky my dad's got solid reflexes."

Sam stopped, thought for a moment, then signed the email "Maestro." After that he clicked on send. Now all he had to do was wait and see what Cody had to say. The ball was in the daredevil's court.

He glanced at his clock. It was now 1:30 a.m. The rain was letting up. He lifted the corner of the curtain, but the driveway at number six was empty again. The guy must have finished whatever the heck he was doing. Sam was about to shut down his computer when he decided to check out the pictures to see if they had gone through all right. He clicked on "Sent Items" and opened the first message he'd forwarded to Cody. As the pixels arranged themselves before his eyes, Sam's mouth fell open.

He shut the first email and opened the second. Then the third.

All the pictures he'd taken had turned out perfectly — the one through the windshield of the Volvo with the bike coming at them and the two outside with the bike in the middle of the road.

Everything was exactly as Sam had remembered it. Every single last detail. The motion. The movement. The position. Everything except the actual bike. The bike in these photos wasn't retro at all. Kronan wasn't written on the crossbar, no mousetrap contraption on the back, no huge fenders, no funny handlebars.

These photos were all of a plain modern mountain bike.

CHAPTER NINE

"Ichabod Crane …"

Sam was sitting at the back of the English class, his head resting in his hand. His eyes were closed. He was exhausted from not sleeping much the previous night. But the teacher's words jolted him upright in his chair.

"… was a tall and gangly schoolmaster living in a secluded glen known as Sleepy Hollow …"

Sam shook away the cobwebs. *Unbelievable! This is it! The story I was thinking about!*

"Seeing as we have our very own Sleepy Hollow, complete with spooky legends, evil curses, and ghostly sightings right here in good ol' Ringwood —" Cate Wolfe's dark eyes narrowed, adding a hint of mystery to her claim "— I thought Washington Irving's short story would be a perfect way to begin the semester." She reached for a huge stack of photocopies, and amid a chorus of groans, began handing them out.

When Sam received his package, he counted the pages. "Eighteen? Single-spaced? And she calls this *short*!"

In the past Sam would never have dreamed of shouting in class, but since he was determined to break free from his old image, he thought it was a pretty good start. He got a few chuckles.

As Ms. Wolfe droned on and on about description, dialogue, and story arches —whatever those were — Sam couldn't help thinking about what she'd said. There were *spooky legends* and *evil curses* surrounding Sleepy Hollow. As a new resident of the eerie place, and what with all the strange things that were happening, he didn't much like the sound of that.

"Well, Mr. Barns, how good of you to join us," Ms. Wolfe said as the classroom door swung open.

Grinning, Cody swaggered to the teacher's desk and handed her a pink late slip. Then he ambled down the aisle and dropped into a seat beside Sam at the back of the class. Raising his eyebrows, he nodded once at Sam approvingly.

He must have seen the pictures!

Sam had been disappointed when Cody wasn't on the bus that morning. Now he'd finally get the chance to clear up the mystery. He rehearsed the conversation in his mind.

Hey, Maniac, you know those pictures I took of your bike? Well, I didn't exactly take them of your bike. I took them of someone else's bike doing the exact same thing, at the exact same spot, on the exact same day. Thing is, your *bike is the one that ended up in my computer and that other bike is, well,* nowhere ...

Sam shook his head. No good. No matter how he tried to rephrase it, it came out sounding ridiculous. As if he was some kind of raving lunatic. There was no way he could ask Cody about the bike. But ... he *could* ask him more about the stunt.

Anxiously, he waited throughout the teacher's lengthy lesson on point of view, stealing glances at Cody now and then. The guy's face was as blank as a sheet of white paper.

"For homework," Ms. Wolfe said finally, "read the first five pages of the story up to the part where Ichabod first meets the lovely Katrina Van Tassel." She surveyed the rows with sharp eyes and a smug smile. "I'd assign you more, but I'm afraid some of you might find the language a bit challenging, given the story was originally published in 1820."

Sam took a quick look at the first page:

In the bosom of one of those spacious coves which indent the eastern shore of the Hudson, at that broad expansion of the river denominated by the ancient Dutch naviga-tors the Tappan Zee, and where they always prudently shortened sail, and implored the

protection of St. Nicholas when they crossed,
there lies a small market-town or rural port,
which by some is called Greensburgh …

He sighed. Ms. Wolfe wasn't kidding. The first sentence went on forever, and there were words Sam didn't know how to pronounce, let alone understand. Bosom *not* being one of them. He smiled to himself.

The bell rang shortly after, and the teacher dismissed the class. Sam gathered his things slowly, watching Cody out of the corner of his eye. He had history next, but he was hoping Cody would speak to him about the pictures first. Maybe they would even start hanging together. But Cody didn't seem remotely interested. He didn't even look at Sam. He just scooped up his binder and followed the crowd toward the doorway where Javon and AJ were waiting.

AJ looked especially pretty today. She wore skinny jeans and a long leopard-print T-shirt and smiled at Sam through the crowd of people. He smiled back. Then Cody arrived at the door, and the three friends disappeared into the hall.

Sam's heart sank. The pictures had been his only shot. For a moment he thought he should race up to Cody and say something, but in the back of his mind he heard Mike's voice telling him to chill. The classroom cleared quickly, and Sam found himself alone with the teacher.

"Can I help you?" Ms. Wolfe asked, noticing Sam lingering near her desk.

Sam cleared his throat. "Uh ... yeah." He fumbled for the right words. "I, uh ... I was wondering, if uh ... maybe you could tell me more about the spooky legends."

"The legends about *our* Sleepy Hollow?"

"Yeah, those."

Ms. Wolfe shook her head. "Sorry. Can't help you there — Sam, isn't it?" She tucked a stray strand of hair behind her ear. "I just moved to town. I've heard the odd murmuring about that place. Some say Sleepy Hollow's haunted. Cursed. But I haven't found anyone who could give me any specifics."

Haunted? Cursed?

Sam swallowed the lump in his throat. He eyed the teacher steadily as his pulse raced. It was probably all garbage. It had to be. Still, he couldn't shake the uneasy feeling he got just thinking about all the weird stuff that had been happening since he'd moved here.

"If you're really interested, why not find some elderly person?" she suggested. "You know how old people like to tell stories."

Sam smiled weakly. "Sure."

"First five pages ..." he heard Ms. Wolfe call as he exited the classroom.

In the hall Sam was surprised to see Cody, Javon, and AJ still hanging around.

"Hey, Maestro," Cody said, raising his chin, "thanks, man."

"No worries." Sam willed himself to appear blasé, though he was pretty excited they had waited for him. He dropped his backpack and pretended to rifle through it for something. The last thing he wanted was to look too eager.

"Whaddya got now, Maestro?" Cody asked.

Yes! Excitement pulsed through Sam's veins. "History," he said, forcing himself not to look up.

"Yo, we're kickin' it in the caf. Wanna come hang?"

Skip class? It was only the second day of school — his dad would kill him if he got caught! The old Sam would never have dared.

"Sure," he said, surprised to hear the word slipping so easily off his tongue. He picked up his backpack and slung it over his shoulder. "Lemme just throw some books into my locker and pick up my math text."

Sam didn't say another word as the four walked through the halls. Cody had his arm around AJ, but more than once Sam caught her glancing in his direction. He opened his locker, stuffed his history textbook inside, and grabbed his math book. Javon was goofing around. He took a running start and leaped over a guy bending in the hall to tie a shoelace.

"Javon Willis!" a deep voice boomed. "No hurdling in the hallway."

Sam saw a short, husky balding man in a grey suit staring coldly at Javon.

"Yo, Mr. G.," Cody said. "Javon can't help it. He's got mad hops."

The man in the grey suit glared at Cody. "What are you and your friends up to, Mr. Barns? Skipping class?"

Sam gulped. This was it. He'd get caught for sure.

Cody's eyes widened innocently. "Skipping? Who, moi? Nah, Mr. G. We've got spares. You can check."

The man flushed slightly. "Count on it, Barns."

Sam breathed a sigh of relief as the man turned and strode down the hallway, disappearing into an office. "Who was that?" he asked as they headed to the cafeteria.

"That's our lovely principal, Mr. Gordon," AJ said. "He's got it in for Cody. Their fathers used to be enemies or something."

Sam shook his head. He had to get used to small-town life. He'd had no idea what it was like to live in a place where everybody knew one another, where the sins of the father were passed down to the son.

In the cafeteria Sam bought a plate of fries drowned in gravy and a can of pop. Cody paid for himself and AJ, but he came up short at the cash register, so Sam tossed him a buck. Things were working out perfectly.

"Cool blog," Sam said as they sat down.

Cody shoved some fries into his mouth. "Uh-huh."

Javon raised an eyebrow. "*Cool?* It's outta control. He gets a hundred hits a day at least."

AJ shot a look at Sam and rolled her eyes. Clearly, she wasn't as impressed with Cody's stunts as Javon was.

"So what exactly were you trying to do with that bike?" Sam asked, easing the conversation toward the mysterious pictures.

"Not much. Just a bit of old school ghost riding," Cody said. "I wanted to see how far the bike would get. J-Man couldn't make it, so I had no one to take any digital pix for my blog. You saved me, man."

Old school ghost riding? Sam wondered what Cody meant by *old school.* Was there a new school type of ghost riding?

"Hope I didn't wreck your bike when I tossed it onto the shoulder," Sam said.

Cody shrugged. "Nah. It's a piece of junk."

Sam was about to ask what kind of bike it was when he felt shivers creep up his spine. He had that same eerie feeling he'd had the other day — the sensation that he was being watched. Slowly, he peered over his shoulder.

The cafeteria was fairly quiet, since first lunch didn't begin until next period. A few guys were playing cards at a table in the far end. A group of girls were talking and laughing across from him. One or two students were scattered here and there, doing homework, reading books, listening to music.

Sam kept one eye on Cody. He could see the blogger's lips moving, but he wasn't listening to a word the guy was saying. AJ was smiling at him again, but Sam was too focused on who might be watching him to smile back. He nodded at Cody mechanically. Cody kept talking. Sam nodded again, still scanning the area for anything out of the ordinary.

"Cool," Cody announced, taking a swig of pop. "So let us know where to meet you."

Huh? Sam's attention snapped back to Cody and Javon. *What's he saying? What have I agreed to?* "Uh … *meet* me?"

"Don't be messin' with us, man," Javon said. "You either wanna come along or you don't. Make up your mind."

AJ's expression was wrinkled into a question. The last thing he wanted to do was disappoint her in any way.

"Sure. Course I wanna go." The words shot out of his mouth before he had time to ponder what he was getting himself into. "I was just multi-tasking, man. Tell me about it again. I didn't catch that last part."

"It's gonna be a hot stunt," Javon said. "Real outta hand."

Sam didn't like the mischief in Javon's eyes. "Stunt? What kind of stunt exactly?"

Javon and Cody grinned at each other.

"You'll see, man," Cody said. "Just tell us where you live and we'll meet you Saturday after midnight."

Sam gazed at the ceiling and took a deep breath. *After midnight? What have I gotten myself into?*

Windows lined the upper hallway and looked into the cafeteria. Sam was suddenly drawn to the farthest window. Walter was standing there, staring right down at him. Sam shivered.

CHAPTER TEN

The next two days were a blur. It was as if Walter had dropped off the face of the planet. He wasn't on the bus either morning, and Sam didn't catch him lurking or spying around any corners. Something was definitely off with the guy. Sam was more than happy that he had disappeared for the time being.

He hung around with Cody, Javon, and AJ during lunch each day, but no one would divulge any more details about the late-night adventure they were planning.

"It'll be the rush of your life, Maestro" was all Cody said. "Meet us on the Tenth Line. On the side of the road under the old willow."

Part of Sam was happy he'd made a few friends — one female one in particular — but the other part was thinking it was going to be short-lived. He kept worrying they'd drop him instantly if he backed out of the stunt, so he played along, acting as if he couldn't wait. All the while, though, he found himself getting more and more frantic. *What if they want me to jump off the roof of the school, or something dumb like that? How am I going to get myself out of it?* He desperately hoped the stunt would just be something stupid but harmless.

At home Miranda was being far too nice, which made Sam wonder what she was up to. Whenever his sister was this sweet, it meant she wanted something. Still, he did his best not to push her buttons. The last thing he needed was to attract any unnecessary attention from his parents.

"How are things going, Sam?" his mother asked when he arrived home from school on Friday. She was sitting in the living room across from the kitchen, watching the news channel.

He shrugged. "All right, I guess." He grabbed a pear from the kitchen counter and threw himself onto the couch opposite her.

"How's your school work coming along? What are you working on?"

Sam had tons of homework for the weekend, including three pages of math, a science test to study for, the rest of "The Legend of Sleepy Hollow" to read, and a one-page summary of the story to write. "Bunch of stuff. Nothing too interesting." He bit into the pear.

Elizabeth reached for the remote and turned off the TV. She frowned at her son. "Are you okay, Sam? Have you made any friends yet?"

Sam flushed. What an insult! *Of course*, he'd made friends. It was as if his mother still thought of him as that awkward little kid nobody liked. He had to set her straight.

"Sure. A few." He took another bite of pear. "One guy, Javon Willis. A girl, AJ. And another guy, Cody Barns. They're really cool."

Sam's father popped up in the doorway. "*Barns?* Did you say *Barns?*"

He was wearing a toque, gloves, and a heavy sweatshirt. His eyes were dark and sunken. The skin on his face was pale and drawn. Sam was alarmed by his appearance.

"Are you, uh, okay, Dad? No offence, but you look horrible."

"Never mind how I look. Just answer the question."

Sam froze. He swallowed a chewed-up piece of pear. He couldn't remember the last time his father had barked at him like that. *Just because he's sick doesn't give him the right to go off on me like that.* Sam wanted to yell something back, swear, or do something worse, but instead he willed himself to be calm. Suddenly, he was really looking forward to Saturday night.

"Yeah, uh, Barns. He's my new friend, Cody."

His father paced and muttered to himself. "Barns, Barns ... can't be. It's a common name."

Sam and his mother exchanged curious glances.

Robert stopped pacing and fixed his glassy eyes on Sam. "Where does this Cody live? What street?"

"I dunno." When his father seemed to get more agitated, he added, "He gets on the bus at the corner of Elm Street and Arlen Avenue."

As soon as those words were out of Sam's mouth, it was as if he'd taken a swing at his father or something. The man stomped around the room, ranting and raving about how *no son of his was going to be friends with no Barns kid*. And if Sam didn't obey, he'd be grounded for life.

Obey? Sam clamped his teeth. *He's treating me like I'm some kind of animal.*

Sam's mother tried to diffuse the situation. "It's all right, honey. Sam's got a good head on his shoulders. I trust him. If he thinks this boy is okay —"

Robert waved one hand furiously. "He's too young to know what's okay and what's not okay. Don't you get it? Looks are deceiving. First you think people are nice, next thing you know, they're forcing you to do things you really don't want to do. Crazy things. Stupid things. Things with horrible consequences. Things that will haunt you for the rest of your life!"

Sam's jaw dropped. Could his father possibly know what he and Cody were up to? Did his father plant some sort of bug on him? Have some kind of nanny cam set up in his room? Was he spying on him? Reading his email? Tracking his computer activity? *How could he possibly know?*

"Calm down, dear," his mother said to her husband. "You're really not well. You need some rest. Why don't you go and have a nap?"

Robert frowned and took a deep breath. He looked at his wife, then at Sam. "Just stay away from that Barns boy, you hear me?"

Sam nodded once. His father stared at him for a few more seconds, then headed upstairs.

As soon as his father was out of sight, he jumped off the sofa. "He treats me like I'm five years old!"

"Sam," his mother almost whispered, "I'm starting to worry about your father. He hasn't been himself lately. He's always freezing. He can't seem to shake this flu and he's refusing to go to the doctor."

Ever since they had moved into the old house, Sam had noticed his dad acting increasingly strange. And that never happened with Robert MacLean. Everything about his father was clockwork. Cut and dried. And his dad was never sick. *Never.* Still, a stupid cold didn't give him the right to attack Sam like that. And why? For making a *friend?*

What made matters worse, was that Sam desperately wanted to talk to his dad about the weird red bike, especially since his father was the only other person who had seen it. Sam needed to make sure it had actually been there — otherwise he'd have to consider that he was hallucinating. But there was no way he could speak to his dad now. The best thing to do was to avoid him for the time being. Avoid him at all cost.

———

> Another of his sources of fearful pleasure was, to pass long winter evenings with the old Dutch wives, as they sat spinning by the fire, with a row of apples roasting and sputtering along the hearth, and listen to their marvelous tales of ghosts and goblins, and haunted fields, and haunted brooks, and haunted bridges, and haunted houses, and particularly of the headless horseman, or galloping Hessian of the Hollow, as they sometimes called him.

"Man," Sam said to himself. "Can this Irving guy write a sentence that *isn't* a thousand words long?"

He was stretched across his bed reading. It was almost 10:00 p.m. when his phone vibrated. "Hey," he said, "what's doin'?"

"Nothin'. You?"

Mike and Sam could say heaps without saying anything at all.

That Washington Irving dude should take lessons from us, thought Sam. *His story would have been half as long.*

"Doing my homework. Are they piling it on you guys, too?"

"Pretty much," Mike said. "Hey, listen, I think I can get my dad to drive me up there tomorrow."

"Uh … tomorrow?"

Thoughts zipped through Sam's mind at lightning speed. It would be great to see Mike, but he couldn't cancel on Cody, either. Cody would think Sam was chickening out and that would be the end of their friendship and his reputation. On the other hand, Mike was a cool guy. If he came along, he'd make Sam look good in front of Cody and Javon, and most important, in front of AJ. But could he count on Mike to go along with the goofy — possibly dangerous — stunt? Sam was about to tell Mike everything when another call came in.

"Hang on." He put Mike on hold and took the other call.

"Hey, Maestro."

It was Cody.

Perfect timing, thought Sam. "What's up, man?"

"You still in for tomorrow night?"

"Sure. Why? What's up?"

"Nothing. Just checking. I don't want to waste my time heading all the way up the Tenth Line if you're gonna back out."

"I don't back out of things. I'll be there. Midnight, right?"

"Midnight," Cody said.

Mike was back on the phone. "So what do you think? Should I ask my dad?"

"Sure." Sam had decided not to tell Mike what was up. It would be better to fill him in on the details in person.

"Great. What's the address again?"

Sam sighed. "Number four Sleepy Hollow Lane."

Mike laughed. "Oh, right, like that horror movie."

"Ghost story."

"Whatever. I'll get my dad to do a Google map. We'll shoot for four o'clock."

"Call me if you get lost in some cow field."

Mike laughed.

Sam pressed end. He sat motionless on his bed for a while, contemplating his situation. On one hand, he was happy he was going to see Mike. On the other hand, he'd pretty much resigned himself to the fact that Mike wasn't going to be in his life a whole heck of a lot anymore — at least not until Sam got his driver's licence. Mike visiting so soon was a bit like pulling off a Band-Aid prematurely and ripping the scab off with it. The old wound was fresh once again as all Sam's anger and resentment for leaving his friend and the neighbourhood he loved gushed back.

He stared at the papers on his bed. Sleepy Hollow. Who would ever want to live in a dumb place like that or this one? He snatched the story and whipped it across the room. The pages flopped into a mess on the floor. Two words caught his eye: *Ichabod Crane.*

Suddenly, Sam found himself thinking about Walter.

CHAPTER ELEVEN

Panic seized Sam's throat with both hands and squeezed. He was running. He was in the middle of a forest and he was racing.

The branches were thick and tangled. The path was barely visible through a crimson fog that hung like a ghostly shroud in the air. Needles tore at his skin as he scrambled blindly, ducking limbs and low-hanging vines.

It's coming!

Sam gasped for air. His lungs felt as if they were going to explode. His heart pounded against his ribs. A searing pain forced his hand to his side, but he couldn't stop. It was after him. Chasing him. He didn't dare glance back, but he knew it was there. He could hear the crunch of leaves close behind. He could feel icy breath against his neck.

It was almost on top of him.

Sam's eyes popped open. He was drenched in sweat. Quickly, he scanned his surroundings. Relief rippled through his body. He was safe in his room. Morning light melted through a gap in the drapes. A lone crow complained outside his bedroom window. The *squawk-squawk* sounded urgent.

He kicked at the covers, swung his legs over the side of the bed, and sat up. With his elbows resting on his knees, Sam held his head in his hands. He took several long, drawn-out breaths to calm his speeding pulse.

He'd had the nightmare before, only this time it had been so clear and vivid. And unlike before, he was able to remember bits and pieces of it. He had been running from something, and though he couldn't remember actually seeing what it was, he knew it was horrible.

Sam rubbed the sleep from his eyes and shook his head. His gaze fell on the heap of pages lying on the floor exactly where he'd tossed them the previous night.

It's that rotten story. It's getting to me.

He grabbed a pair of jeans and a T-shirt from the pile of laundry on the floor, pulled them on, and headed downstairs.

His mother and sister were just leaving. It was Miranda's first day at her new dance studio, and they wanted to get her signed up before classes began. After that they were going to check out the town and do some grocery shopping, which would leave Sam alone with his dad most of the day. Sam sat by himself in the kitchen. He wolfed down a bowl of cereal and hurried back to his room. His father's mood hadn't improved whatsoever, so he wanted to stay clear of him.

In his room Sam switched on his computer and opened the file with the pictures he'd taken. Maximizing the photo of the bike gliding down the hill toward the Volvo, he examined it closely. There was nothing unusual about it. Nothing out of the ordinary. Just a plain mountain bike.

Sam puzzled over the image for a few minutes before navigating to Cody's blog. The frothy Doberman's jowls greeted him. There was a new entry:

> Maestro learns how to stunt ... detes to follow ...
>
> Posted: September 7, 10:30 p.m.

Two comments were posted. One from Homegirl:

> Oh, please tell me you ain't gonna school that boy in the fine art of being a fool? Or ... you got something else in mind?
>
> Posted: September 7, 10:31 p.m.

The other comment was from J-Man:

Homegirl's got a fat mouth she may wanna
shut before someone shuts it for her.

Posted: September 7, 10:49 p.m.

Sam sat back in his chair. Something about Javon's words didn't seem right. Was he telling Homegirl off for calling Cody a fool? Or was it something else?

The crow outside started to squawk again.

CHAPTER TWELVE

Sam spent most of Saturday waiting for Mike and trying to avoid his father. He hung out in his room, did some math homework, and studied a bit for his science test.

He had been pretty relaxed all morning, but as afternoon set in, he started to get nervous. What was Cody planning on having them do? What role would Sam have to play? The more he thought about it the happier he was that Mike was coming. With Mike there Sam wouldn't feel as if it was a two-against-one situation. Mike being there would more or less balance things out.

At a quarter to four the doorbell echoed through the hallway.

"Dude," Sam said as Mike and his father stepped inside.

Mike dropped his sleeping bag and scanned the entrance floor to ceiling. "Cool digs."

"Bit of a change, eh, Sam?" Mike's father said. "How are you enjoying life in the country?"

Sam shrugged. "Okay, I guess."

"Hey, Mr. McLean," Mike said as Sam's father appeared at the top of the stairs, wearing a thick wool sweater.

"Hello, Mike." Sam's father sounded more cheerful than he had in days. "Glad you could drive him up, Jack. I know it's a bit of a hike, but this will be good for Sam. He's been miserable without Mike."

Sam gritted his teeth. *Did he have to say that?* It made Sam sound like such a loser.

"No problem," Jack said. He turned to his son. "I'll pick you up early tomorrow afternoon."

"Thanks, Jack," Robert said. "I'd drive him home, but I've had a bit of a cold this past week."

"No worries, Robert. Old house a bit drafty?"

Sam watched a shadow creep across his father's face. "Right ... see you tomorrow, Jack."

After shutting the front door, Sam hustled Mike into the family room as quickly as possible to avoid his father saying any more weird or embarrassing things. In the state he was in there was no telling what would fly out of his mouth.

Sam felt odd seeing his best friend. It had only been eight days, yet it already seemed like a lifetime since they'd hung together. Mike broke the awkward silence first and updated Sam about school and the neighbourhood. Sam listened and nodded but felt disconnected from everything. Next it was Sam's turn. He started to tell Mike about Cody and Javon and the midnight stunt when his mother and Miranda returned home. Sam and Mike helped them unpack the groceries, talking and laughing superficially as they got the food and supplies sorted out and put away.

After grabbing a huge bag of Doritos and a couple of cans of pop, Sam said to his mother, "We'll be in my room." Then he eyed Miranda with a look that said: *And you'd better not bug us.*

Miranda opened her mouth to say something, then glanced at Mike and decided to close it again. She turned her back indignantly.

Sam's room was in its usual state of disarray. Mike waded through the piles of clothing and threw himself onto Sam's bed. "You trying out for the slob-of-the-year award?"

"You're too funny." Sam tossed the bag of Doritos to Mike, who snatched it out of the air with one hand and popped it open.

Mike shovelled a handful of chips into his mouth, then said, "Don't bother trying out for the football team. You throw like your sister."

Sam gave him a can of pop. "At least I don't wear my sister's clothes."

"Whaddya mean?" Mike sat up and pulled at his T-shirt. "Purple's in, man." He feigned a hurt look.

The awkwardness between them, Sam thought, was melting away. Things were beginning to feel like the good ol' days.

Sam sat at his computer and navigated to Cody's blog. "Hey, check this out. It's really cool."

Mike joined him and watched as the foaming Doberman appeared. "*Maniac Stunts?* What's that all about?"

"It's great. It's my friend Cody's blog. Check this out. He does all these cool stunts." Sam displayed all the crazy pictures of Cody doing wild stunts. "So what do you think?"

"I think there's a village somewhere missing its idiot."

Sam rolled his eyes. "Seriously, man. These stunts are hot."

"Whatever." Mike crammed more chips into his mouth.

Clearly, this conversation wasn't going as planned. Still, Sam had to tell Mike what was going to happen at some point, so that might as well be now. "Listen, tonight Cody's got something really cool planned. We're gonna sneak out and meet him at midnight by the old willow tree. It'll be a blast."

Mike didn't say anything at first. He ate some more chips, then swiped his hand across his jeans and dragged his finger across the mouse pad on the laptop to scroll back to Cody's blog. He examined the pictures more closely.

Sam was getting nervous. He had to up the ante. "There's a girl, too. She's pretty hot. She's sort of Cody's girl, but I think she likes me." For a moment Sam thought Mike wasn't going to go along with the plan.

"Midnight, eh? Okay. Cool."

Relief washed over Sam. This was perfect.

"But, Sam, dude," Mike added, "you don't want to mess with someone else's girl."

"I'm not messing with her. I just think she's hot."

Mike eyed him suspiciously. "If you say so. But let's make one thing clear. I'm not jumping off a roof or anything. Got it?" Mike shuffled back to the bed and cracked open his pop. "I've got basketball tryouts next week. I'm not screwing that up for some stupid stunt."

Sam couldn't have been happier. Everything was going to be awesome. "Speaking of basketball, let's play some one-on-one before dinner."

They headed outside and tossed a few hoops. The sun was already low in the sky, bathing Sleepy Hollow in a tawny glow. Sam was driving to the basket when he caught a glimpse of Walter staring down at them from an upper window in the house next door. He missed his shot, and Mike grabbed the rebound.

"Don't look now," Sam whispered, jerking his head toward the window, "but there's that geeky guy I was telling you about."

Mike looked up. "Where?"

Sam swung around, his eyes darting to the neighbours' window, but Walter had vanished again.

CHAPTER THIRTEEN

The immediate cause, however, of the preva-
lence of supernatural stories in these parts,
was doubtless owing to the vicinity of Sleepy
Hollow. There was a contagion in the very
air that blew from that haunted region; it
breathed forth an atmosphere of dreams and
fancies infecting all the land.

"I can't believe you have to read this junk," Mike
said.

It was 11:25 p.m., and everyone had gone to bed
ages ago. Sam and Mike were goofing around, wasting
time until midnight.

"I've still got five and a half pages to read before
Monday, but the thing keeps putting mc to sleep." Sam
tossed the booklet aside and powered up his phone.
"Want to play Bubble Buster?"

As they alternated games, Sam kept one eye on the
clock. They had to make their move in the next fifteen

minutes. Sam couldn't risk being late and have Cody think he'd backed out. As the seconds ticked away, Sam's palms began to sweat. He really didn't know Cody and Javon that well, and he had no idea what they had in store for him. What if they were going to make him do something really dangerous? What if his father was right?

So what if he's right? thought Sam. *I'm sick of living my life according to his perfect plan. I need to make my own decisions. My own mistakes. If this is a mistake, it's mine to make.* He took a deep breath and steadied his nerves. *And besides, I've got Mike with me ...*

At a quarter to twelve Sam tucked his cell into his pocket and pulled on a thick sweatshirt and a black toque. "Let's do it."

Mike, who was practically asleep in his bag on the floor, stood, yawned, and stretched. He grabbed Sam in a headlock and rubbed his knuckles against Sam's skull. "You look like you're all set to rob a bank."

Sam broke free. "Shut up! You'll wake up my parents."

Mike grinned. "Okay, okay."

Sam crept to the door. The upper and lower hallways were dark and quiet. He gestured to Mike, and they slid out of the bedroom and snuck down the stairs. The old floorboards groaned once or twice under their weight. Each time they creaked, Sam and Mike froze and waited a few seconds. Then, when they were certain all was quiet, they continued.

There was something Sam didn't like about the old house. A creepy feeling he got. As if someone were watching him. The sensation was magnified at night so that he found himself checking the shadows, searching left and right, up and down, as he tiptoed through the darkness.

Sam clicked the deadbolt, and with steady hands, opened the door wide enough to slip through. His heart fluttered as he pulled the old oak door shut as gently as possible.

Made it, Sam thought.

The air outside was damp and cold. Sam shivered once before stepping into the amber glow of the lone street lamp. All seven houses were dark. Everything was still.

They moved swiftly along the road toward the tunnel of branches. The rubber soles of their running shoes produced a mesmerizing rhythm as they gripped the pavement.

In the daytime the tunnel of trees was dark, but now it was pitch-black. Sam looked at what should have been patches of sky. Everything was dark. *New moon,* he thought to himself. As he ducked into the tunnel, he couldn't see his hand in front of his face.

"This way," Sam whispered. He could barely make out Mike, who was only a metre or so away. Sam nearly jumped out of his skin when the shrill cry of a screech owl sliced through the silence.

"Dude, relax," Mike said.

Sam had to get a grip on himself. He couldn't let Cody see how nervous he was, or AJ for that matter.

The old weeping willow was just ahead, a black silhouette against the charcoal-grey of the open field beyond. Its hanging branches were so thick they were almost trunks of separate trees forming a kind of monstrous cage. Sam picked up his pace. The main road and open fields past the willow would put his mind at ease.

They were almost under the old tree when a shadow sprang from behind the trunk. Sam's heart nearly leaped into his throat. His knees turned to jelly.

"Yo, Maestro," Cody called. "What took you?"

"You said midnight," Sam said a little peevishly. He hoped Cody didn't notice he was catching his breath.

"Midnight. *The Witching Hour. Bhwahaha!*" Cody slapped Sam upside the head and then began humming a pathetic rendition of B-rated horror movie music.

Mike stepped forward.

"Who's this guy?" Cody demanded, clearly taken aback by Mike's sudden appearance.

"This is, uh, Mike. He's up from Toronto."

Cody remained silent, as if he were trying to calculate a really tough math problem.

Sam started to think Mike might have been right. *Lost: one idiot. Return to village immediately.*

"Where's AJ?" Sam asked, looking around hopefully. "And Javon," he added quickly when he saw Mike give him the eye.

"AJ's not coming. She doesn't like me doing stunts. Gets too worried about me. You know how it is."

"Right," Sam said, trying to keep the disappointment out of his voice.

"So, you cool with stunts … *Mikey Mouse?*" Cody asked, taking a step forward.

"That's good," Mike said. "Really good. Take you long to think it up?"

"Shut your mouth, city rat!" Cody growled.

Oh-oh. Nothing seemed to be going the way Sam had planned. AJ was supposed to be here, and Cody and Mike should be hitting it off, not about to kill each other.

"Come on, guys," Sam said. "Be cool. This stunt's gonna be a blast. Right, Cody?"

Mike and Cody stared at each other, neither saying a word.

"Where's Javon?" Sam asked, still trying to defuse the situation. He scanned the darkness, half expecting another figure to jump out at him, but in that instant, as though in response to his question, the sound of an ignition ripped through the silence and a set of headlights switched on, illuminating the old willow and its three prisoners.

Who's in that car? Sam wondered. *And what's it doing here?* But when Cody laughed and clapped him on the back, he knew it could only mean one thing.

The driver's door opened, and a dark figure emerged. The headlights were fiercely bright, so all Sam could see was the shadow of a lean figure with broad shoulders and a toque perched high on his head.

"Let's roll!" Javon said.

Cody shoved Sam toward the car. He could see Javon clearly now. The guy was grinning like a madman. Sam hadn't thought for a moment that the stunt would involve a car. He eyed the old Honda Accord. The black paint was covered in rust patches. The tinted windows were peeling, and even in the darkness the tires looked practically bald.

Sam glanced over his shoulder. Mike hadn't moved an inch. He was still standing under the willow tree, arms crossed. "Come on, Mike, let's go." But Mike ignored him.

"Forget him, man," Cody said, giving Sam another push toward the car.

Sam pulled away and turned. "What's up, Mike? Let's go."

Mike half smiled. "You kidding me? I'm not getting in that piece of junk with those idiots."

Sam couldn't believe this was happening. His world was crumbling. Mike was supposed to make him seem cool, not leave him dangling like this.

"*Mmm* ... do I smell KFC?" Cody said. "Forget the chicken, Maestro. Let's go."

Sam took a few steps backward toward Mike. "What's your problem?"

Mike shook his head. "There's no way that guy has a driver's licence. Do you have any idea what you could be getting yourself into? I'm telling you, these guys aren't worth it."

Sam moved closer and dropped his voice. "Why are you bailing on me? I thought you were my friend."

"Dude, this is bad news. You do whatever you want, but I'm outta here."

"Hey, girls!" Cody shouted. "What's the deal? You going for a manicure or are you riding with us?"

Sam glanced back at Cody, then at Mike. His head was pounding. His brain was telling him Mike was right. But so what? Mike lived worlds away. If Sam was lucky, he'd see Mike once a month. He'd have to see Cody and Javon every day. If he went with them, they'd accept him.

If he didn't, they'd make life at school a living hell. AJ would think he was a total geek. Why couldn't Mike just go along? Why did he have to make such a big deal? If he was such a good friend, he'd know what this meant to Sam. If he was such a good friend, he'd go along. Mike was abandoning Sam when he needed him most. Easy for Mike — he had nothing to lose. He still had friends. He wasn't the one who would have to face Cody, Javon, AJ, and the whole freakin' school on Monday.

The way Sam saw things now there was only one way to go. Glaring at Mike, he tossed him the house keys. "Leave the door open. And don't bother waiting up." He turned and walked toward Cody, who jabbed him in the arm.

"I'm totally stoked, man," Cody said. "Are you stoked?"

"Uh, yeah, sure. *Stoked.*" Sam peered over his shoulder. Mike was watching him. "Whose car is it?" he asked, willing his voice to sound as casual as possible.

Javon laughed. "You worry too much, Maestro."

Sam stuck out his chin. "Who said I was worried? I was just asking. I didn't know you even had a driver's licence."

Cody snorted. "You're too funny, Maestro. Driver's licence! Good one!"

CHAPTER FOURTEEN

The wheels burned rubber as Javon threw the Accord into gear and slammed his foot hard on the gas. The car took off and sailed up the deserted Tenth Line, taking the potholes and bumps like a jet-ski crashing over waves.

Cody, who was riding shotgun, cranked up the volume of the radio, blasting a rap song that Sam had never heard before into the night air. Sam reached over and yanked his seat belt, but Cody, looking back, yelled, "Won't do ya no good, Maestro! You'll be taking it off soon enough."

Sam managed a weak smile but snapped the buckle in place all the same. *Are we going to street-race? Is that what this is about?* He had a sinking feeling in his stomach. Mike was right. This was bad news.

"Cool music," Sam said above the thudding base.

"It's sick, man!" Javon agreed.

The car was going way too fast, and Sam was getting really worried. He tapped his foot nervously. He'd seen enough news reports on crazy teen driving gone wrong. Still, he forced himself to sound casual. "So, uh, who is it?"

Cody looked at Sam and rolled his eyes. "You been listening to that classical junk again? Don't you know I-90 when you hear him?"

"Right, I-90. Sure, I know him. So what exactly is this stunt? I mean, what are we gonna do?" Sam rubbed his fingertips nervously. His palms were sweating.

Cody and Javon exchanged grins.

"Don't get yourself all knotted up," Cody said. "Chill. You got your phone, Maestro? You ready to get me some good pictures? And you can make a video, right? I wanna upload a vlog."

Take pictures? A short video? Is that all he wants me to do? Sam breathed deeply and let the air out slowly. *I can take pictures. No problem.* Sam's pulse was finally slowing down when Javon yanked the wheel hard and pressed his foot to the floor. The tires shrieked as the car spun around, doing a doughnut in the middle of the road. Then they took off again, heading back toward town at alarming speed.

As they passed the entrance to Sleepy Hollow, Sam searched for Mike, but he was long gone. For a moment Sam thought about pushing open the door and throwing himself out. It took every ounce of willpower to remain seated. *I'm only taking pictures,* he kept telling himself. *Sit tight and this will all be over soon.*

When they got to the top of the hill where Sam and his father had first seen the riderless bike, Javon hit the brakes and the car screeched to a halt. Cody fiddled with the music, switching tracks until he found the song he wanted. Then Javon put the car into neutral, and they began coasting downhill.

"You ready to ride this whip?" Cody asked as the Accord rolled forward.

Sam still didn't have the foggiest idea what was actually happening, but he dug out his phone and powered it up. "Yeah, man, I gotcha," he said, his voice quavering slightly on the last word.

The music shook the entire car. Two voices rapped alternately — the main guy sang the lyrics, and the other, a deep voice, created a haunting rhythm in the background:

> Ghost ride …
> Ghost ride …

The car moved slowly at first, then began to pick up speed.

> Ghost ride …
> Ghost ride …

Near the bottom of the hill, Cody and Javon opened their windows.

"Let's do it!" Cody shouted. "Let's ghost ride, man!"

They both climbed out of their windows onto the roof of the vehicle. Sam couldn't believe what was happening. *These guys are nuts!*

But before the thought passed from his brain to his lips, he sensed stomping on the roof above him. He opened his window and stuck his head out. *Cody and Javon were dancing on the roof of the gliding car!*

Ghost ride ...
Ghost ride ...
Ghost ride ...

"Boo-yah!" Javon screamed into the night sky.

"Hey, Maestro, get up here!" Cody cried. "Start taking those pictures, man!"

Sam's brain scrambled through the thought process. *What do I do now? I can't go up there. These guys are lunatics! What do I say? How do I get out of this?*

The road had levelled off. The car was travelling at top speed now, but soon it would slow — if they didn't go off the road entirely, Sam thought, as the car drifted into the opposite lane. He unfastened his seat belt, lurched forward, and steadied the wheel. Good thing the road was empty.

"Get up here, Maestro — now!" Cody yelled. "Take the pictures!"

Take pictures. That was it. That was what had gotten him into this mess in the first place. Those pictures. At this exact spot. Those pictures of ...

"I'll bust your grille if you don't get your butt up here right now, Maestro!"

Take a picture, thought Sam. *Just one. Quick. Take a picture and this nightmare will end.* He took a deep breath. Then, clutching his phone, he pulled himself partway out of the car, sitting on the window, gripping the roof with one hand and aiming the cell with the other. Cold wind numbed his face. The road was dark.

Click.

A picture of the top of Cody's head. Sam hit the options key, found Maniac on his list, and pressed send.

Click.

This time he got one of Javon's feet and the roof of the Accord. Again he scrolled down the list of *M*'s, found Maniac, and punched send.

The music was getting to Sam. It seemed to be all around him, inside him.

Ghost ride ...
Ghost ride ...
Ghost ride ...

One more and this would be over. Sam located the video icon and clicked. He began videoing Cody and Javon dancing. The video was perfect. He could see everything. Cody. Javon. The roof of the car. The night sky. Perfect.

Sam fingered the options key and scrolled through the *M*'s. But before he could transmit the video, he caught sight of something. His heart skipped a beat. Lights. A pair of headlights. In the distance. Coming right at them.

The Accord had drifted once again into the opposite lane. They were going to collide head-on.

> Ghost ride …
> Ghost ride …
> Ghost ride …

The headlights were approaching quickly.

Three hundred metres away.

Some idiot with his high beams on. Sam tried, but he couldn't budge. Cody and Javon didn't seem to notice — or care. They were too busy dancing like fools.

Two hundred metres away.

Sam willed himself to yell. He opened his mouth, but no sound emerged. He had to get down and grab the wheel or they were all going to die. He had to move, but he couldn't. He was stuck, immobile in the light that was getting larger. Brighter. Wrapping itself around him. Swallowing him.

Ghost ride ...
Ghost ride ...
Ghost ride ...

The song kept pounding away. Sam couldn't think, couldn't breathe.
One hundred metres away.

Ghost ride ...
Ghost ride ...
Ghost ... ride ghost ... ride ghost ...
Ride ghost ...

The only thing Sam managed to move was his thumb on the send key. He transmitted the video, then shut his eyes and braced himself.

Ride ghost
Ride ...

CHAPTER FIFTEEN

The music stopped. The wind was on Sam's face. He was flying — no, *gliding*. All sense of panic and desperation had evaporated. He was soaring like an eagle, awaiting the impact that never came.

One of his hands gripped the roof of the car and the other his cellphone, but wait, something had changed. Both hands were now wrapped around something completely different. What was it? Bars?

Handlebars.

Sam snapped his eyes open. He couldn't believe what he was seeing. He was dreaming … dreaming or … *dead*.

He was no longer in a car. He was on a bike. An old bike. The one in the photo he'd taken — the *Kronan*. He wasn't wearing a toque, and his arms were different. They felt like someone else's. His clothes weren't the same, either. He was coasting downhill in the middle of the road, all alone, heading toward a pair of headlights that were almost on top of him. Behind him he heard a sound. An engine. And there were lights, as well. Getting brighter. Another vehicle was approaching from behind.

He was trapped.

For a second time he was sure he was going to die. Only this time it didn't seem to matter. It was all so real and yet so dreamlike, as though every move he made wasn't his own, as if he were a stowaway in someone else's mind and body.

Everything unfolded in slow motion.

Sam was going to be sandwiched between the two vehicles. He heard a loud, long horn blast — the vehicle behind him was a truck, an eighteen-wheeler! There was no time to think. He couldn't pull to the right or the left. Either way he'd be hit.

He lifted his arms to shield his eyes. The bike drifted to the right. The wheel wobbled. He was going down, striking the gravel hard, skidding along the road. The exposed skin on his hands and cheek scraped across dirt and rocks. And though he could sense a layer of his skin tearing off, somehow he didn't feel any pain. He was off the road and in the ditch. But it was too late. The damage was done.

Sam watched in horror as the truck jackknifed. The car swerved to avoid the much bigger vehicle and lost control. It went under the eighteen-wheeler in a sickening clash of metal against metal. The car was dragged under the truck until both slammed into the field on the other side of the road. Everything fell silent.

Scrambling to his feet, Sam could see that the car's headlights were still on, slicing through the darkness. He staggered toward the wreckage. The roof of the car had been ripped off like the husk of a ripe ear of corn. The truck was on its side in the ditch. Twisted metal and broken glass lay strewn across the field. The stench of gas and oil was thick in the air.

Sam moved in closer.

Closer.

A leg was sticking out of the truck driver's cab. The roofless car was red — some kind of big old Ford, like the kind he'd seen in his grandfather's old photos. Sam made out two bodies in the front seat. His first instinct was to race to help, but he quickly realized it was no use. The front seat was covered in dark liquid.

Oil?

No, not oil.

The body of a woman lay slumped over the wheel, a twisted, tangled mass. Her face was unrecognizable, but still there was something familiar about her. *The woman's dress.* He'd seen it somewhere before. He reached down and touched her. Blood was everywhere. So much blood. It was on his hands, shirt, jeans. Then his gaze drifted to the figure beside her ...

His eyes were looking at something, but his brain refused to register it. It was right in front of him, but his mind fought his eyes. Suddenly, it clicked, like the last piece of a puzzle, and the image became clear.

Sam's whole body shuddered violently as he stepped back. He'd played a lot of violent video games. Watched a lot of TV crime shows showing autopsies. Saw a lot of news reports. But nothing could have prepared him for this.

Bile rose in his throat. He choked it down, gagging and coughing as he scrambled, stumbling backward. It was as if a huge snake were coiled around his chest. Squeezing. Squeezing. He turned to run, but fell to the ground. He slammed his head against the road, trying to shake loose the image. That image. That horrible, disgusting picture in his mind.

The one passenger. The one beside the woman. *There was nothing but a bloody stump where there should have been a head!*

"Come on, Bobby!" he heard someone shout behind him. "Come on, man. Let's get outta here!"

Whose voice is that? Is that Cody?

It sounded like Cody, but not exactly. Sam lifted his head, but all he could see was a dark shadow.

Who is that? And who is Bobby?

"Come on, man. Grab your bike. We gotta get out of here. We gotta —"

Sam couldn't move. His bones had liquefied.

"Come on!"

The guy was screaming now. Grabbing him by the shoulders. Shaking him. Trying to drag him to his feet.

Sam struggled to get free.

CHAPTER SIXTEEN

"Come on, man! We gotta get outta here!"

Reality hit Sam like a slap in the face. He stopped flailing.

It *was* Cody.

Sam searched wildly. He was lying on his back in the middle of the road and Cody was beside him, trying to yank him to his feet. Only one car was in the ditch — the black Accord. It was right side up and still had its roof. No other cars were around. There was no stench of oil in the night air.

The nightmare hadn't happened. There hadn't been a collision. No bike. No blood. No headless body. It had all been a weird hallucination. When Sam realized he was holding his breath, he let out the air slowly.

"Come on!" shouted Cody, pulling at him again. His voice was high-pitched and desperate. "Don't zone out on me again, Maestro. We gotta get outta here. Quick, before someone sees us!"

Sam felt groggy, as if he were just waking from a long

sleep. He rubbed the back of his head, pushed Cody's hands away with one arm, and stood. When he started walking toward the Honda, Cody grabbed him by the sleeve and swung him around.

"Don't you get it, man?" His voice was part hiss, part squeal. "We gotta get outta here before anyone sees us. We gotta forget this night ever happened. We can't ever talk about this again. Not to anyone ... not even to each other ... not *ever*!"

Sam searched Cody's eyes. There was fear in them. Still feeling only half-awake, Sam tried to comprehend what was happening.

Okay, so the car's in the ditch. It's not the end of the world. Not like the accident I just witnessed — or imagined I'd witnessed. We'll call a tow-truck. What's Cody so freaked out about? The car? It isn't even his. It belongs to —

"Javon ..." Sam whispered. His eyes met Cody's. "Where's Javon?"

Cody didn't answer right away. He stared at Sam, his eyes dark and frightening.

"I said, *where's Javon?*" Sam's heart beat faster. His mouth was dry.

Cody looked at Sam, and then over at the car. "There," he said in a barely audible voice.

Sam's eyes followed Cody's gaze. They zeroed in on

a pair of legs sticking out from beneath the car. Sam's heart exploded. He shoved Cody aside and scuttled toward the vehicle, but Cody caught him, tackled him from behind, and threw him to the ground.

"What are you doing, you idiot?" Sam demanded. "Are you out of your mind? Let me go! We have to help him!"

The two wrestled until Cody pinned Sam. "Don't you get it?" Cody screamed. "I already checked him! He's dead, man. Dead!"

Sam stopped struggling. "You're lying! How can he be dead? What happened?"

"You must have fallen out of the car and smacked your head when we hit that pothole." Cody took deep breath. "Javon fell, too. Only he fell forward and went under the car."

Sam thrashed about, nearly breaking free, but Cody pinned him again. "We gotta call the cops, man. Call an ambulance. Call someone."

"There's nothing we can do for Javon. Let it go, man. We gotta get outta here. No one knows what happened except you and me."

"And Mike ..." Sam whispered.

"Mike don't know nothing! So we drove off with Javon. So what? We'll say we did something else. Some stupid little stunt. Then Javon dropped us off and he drove away on his own. We don't know what happened to him — got it? We weren't with him. That's the story."

Sam couldn't believe what he was hearing. This was crazy. Insane. In one swift motion he knocked Cody off and staggered toward the Honda.

"I'm not going down for this — no way, man!" Cody yelled.

Sam kept moving.

"You're an idiot, Sam!" Cody shouted. It was the first time he'd called him by his name. "We can walk away from this, you and me, or we can go down for something that was an accident. An accident, man! You wanna go to Juvie for an accident?"

Sam stopped. He eyed the lifeless legs. He was battling himself, but he was losing. He didn't want to admit it, but he didn't want to go to Juvie for an accident, either. Tears spilled down his cheeks. He swiped them away bitterly before Cody noticed. "So what do we do? Just leave him here?"

In the distance a pair of headlights appeared. They were about two kilometres away. Sam had to make a decision quickly.

"Let's just get outta here," Cody said. "Someone will find him. No one needs to know we were here. Not Mikey Mouse. Not even AJ. No one."

The lights were approaching rapidly. The car had to

be doing a hundred. Soon it would be on top of them. Would the driver even see the Honda in the darkness? Would he see what was underneath? Or would he speed by, thinking it was an old, abandoned vehicle?

"What's it gonna be, man?" Cody demanded. "Home or prison?"

The car was less than a kilometre away. It was now or never.

Sam scrunched his eyes, took a deep breath, and backed away from the Honda. He ran to the opposite side of the road, with Cody at his heels, and dived into the ditch as the car sped by. Sam glanced up as it passed. It was the blue Mustang.

"So we're cool, right?" Cody asked. "We don't talk about this? Not to *anyone*?"

Sam couldn't bring himself to say a word. He still couldn't believe what he was doing. He pressed his lips together and nodded once. His stomach bubbled and boiled. His mind kept telling him he was making a deal with the devil, but he didn't want to go to jail. The stunt wasn't his idea. He hadn't been the driver. He didn't even really know what happened. But he did know it was an accident. *An accident.*

Walking north, Sam stayed low in the ditch and out of sight. It was a long way home. He heard Cody call behind him, his voice echoing in the distance.

"Remember, man. This is our secret." Sam couldn't bring himself to look back. He never wanted to see Cody again.

Sam kept trudging, keeping to the shadows in the ditch by the road. He couldn't bear to think of what he'd done. It was so horrible that his mind switched off. The damp air seeped into his clothes, making him colder, freezing his brain.

As he hiked, he became acutely aware of every sound around him. A bird screeched in the distance. The wind whistled through the trees. Several times he thought he heard a car approaching. Each time that occurred he dived flat into the damp grass and dirt and waited, only to realize it was his imagination.

Sam began to shiver and hugged himself to stop the tremors. He marched on for almost an hour, his feet heavy, his mind cloudy and dull. His teeth chattered as words slipped through: "Didn't happen ... all a dream ... a dream ..." Several times he stopped to remind himself where he was. His feet led him onward mechanically, dragging his body forward, until nearing the woods that hid Sleepy Hollow he started to convince himself that everything had been just that — a dream.

When Sam entered the tunnel of trees past the old willow, the wind suddenly died off. There was never any wind in Sleepy Hollow. Darkness covered him in a cold blanket. He strained his eyes to see through the tunnel, but it was no use.

Crunch.

Something rustled the leaves. "Mike, is that you?" Sam searched frantically, but he couldn't see a thing. He picked up his pace.

Sam needed to get home. If he could lie in his bed and pull the covers over his head, then this nightmare would fade away. He'd wake up and it would all be a dream. If only he could get home ...

Crunch.

There it was again. Something was moving through the trees. Following him. Sam broke into a sprint. His house wasn't far now.

Crunch, crunch.

Sam ran as fast as he could, peering at the darkness as he hurtled through the tunnel that seemed to close in on him. For a split second he thought he caught sight of a shadow as it slipped behind an old tree trunk.

That shadow.

That shape.

It had no head!

Sam broke through the trees, racing past driveway after driveway. Taking the steps of his porch in one giant leap, he lunged for the front door that Mike had left unlocked. He swung it open and slid inside, shutting it quickly but quietly, and then leaned back on the heavy oak to catch his breath. His heart was pounding. His side was aching.

The house was silent. Sam scanned the darkness. There was an empty feeling about it. He took a step toward the stairs. The old floors creaked beneath his weight, and he stopped. He was sure someone was watching him. Every nerve in his body was taut. Only his eyes moved, examining every corner and crevice.

"Mike?" he whispered.

Someone giggled. It was an airy sound that echoed through the hall.

Sam swung around. "Miranda?"

But there was no one there.

CHAPTER SEVENTEEN

"What happened to you?" Mike asked when Sam entered the bedroom.

Sam halted in his tracks. A sliver of light from the lone street lamp leaked through the gap in the curtains, setting him aglow. His clothes were sopping. His face and hands were muddy.

"N-nothing," he said, averting his eyes. He was shivering, but he forced himself to sound as casual as he could.

"Wow! You look like crap, man. You okay?"

"Yeah, sure. Why wouldn't I be?" Sam pulled off his sweatshirt, tossed it onto the floor, and grabbed a dry T-shirt from a pile of fresh clothes folded on the dresser.

"So what did you and your new friends end up doing?" Mike asked.

Sam didn't like the way Mike emphasized the word *friends*. "What do you care? You bailed on me, remember?"

Mike sighed. "I didn't bail on you, Sam. I just didn't

feel like getting mixed up in anything illegal. I told you not to go —"

"Who are you — *my mother?*"

Anger boiled in the pit of Sam's stomach. He was furious, partly because Mike had abandoned him when he needed his friend most, but also because Mike had been right. Sam should have listened. He should never have gotten into that car with Cody and Javon.

"Dude, chill," Mike said. "I was just —"

"Quit busting my chops! I don't know why you came up here, anyway. You should've stayed home. Some best friend you turned out to be."

Sam didn't know what he was saying anymore. He was out of his mind. His emotions had gone haywire. Fear, panic, anger, anguish — they were writhing like snakes in his gut, twisting and turning until they knotted into a giant ball of confusion. He should be talking to Mike. He should be telling him everything. But he couldn't. He couldn't face himself. Instead, he threw himself onto his bed, closed his eyes, and pretended to sleep.

Mike didn't say another word.

CHAPTER EIGHTEEN

"You look awful," Miranda said when Sam and Mike came downstairs the next morning.

Normally, Sam would have had a million nasty comebacks ready for his sister, but today they were lost in the fog of his brain.

Sam was exhausted. He hadn't slept a wink. His stomach churned. He couldn't bring himself to look his sister in the eye. He felt if he made eye contact with her, with Mike, with anyone, they'd read his face and know his dirty secret.

Just act normal, he told himself. *Nothing happened. Nothing happened …*

Miranda and Mike chatted casually while they ate breakfast. Sam couldn't eat a bite. He sat there, moving the crisp bacon and scrambled eggs around on his plate — the sight of food made him want to heave.

Get a grip. You've gotta act normal …

Sam and Mike had only exchanged a few words, avoiding the topic of the previous night altogether. Mike had called his dad to come and get him early. His father was on his way. He'd be there by noon.

"Where's Dad?" Miranda asked.

"Still can't seem to shake his cold," Sam's mother said. Her expression betrayed her worry. "It's been a week, now. I'm forcing him to go to the walk-in clinic today. It might take a few hours if the clinic is busy, so you guys will be on your own for a while."

Sam and Mike barely spoke for the rest of the morning. They played a few video games, watched a bit of TV, and avoided looking at each other. The tension was excruciating. Sam felt a surge of relief when Mike's father finally arrived.

"So how did it go?" Mike's father asked.

"Great," Mike said, though his tone told a different story.

"Okay ..." Mike's dad said. He must have sensed something was wrong because he didn't press the issue. "See you soon, Sam?"

Sam nodded. "Sure, see you." He forced a slight smile, then shut the door behind them.

Finally, he thought, hauling himself up the stairs and collapsing on his bed. He tried to close his eyes, but sleep wouldn't come. Sam kept thinking he should be doing something. He could do the rest of his homework. Take a shower. Surf the Net. But each time he tried to get up, he sank down again. Everything seemed so totally meaningless.

I've gotta snap out of this. If I don't, they'll know something's wrong.

Sam finally found the strength to force himself to his feet. He pulled on his grey hoodie and grabbed his basketball. He would shoot a few hoops. Maybe that would calm his nerves. Settle his stomach.

The road was a kaleidoscope of yellow, orange, and purple. It was as though, during the night, the trees had come up with some secret plan to shed half their leaves simultaneously. The air in Sleepy Hollow was still. He gazed at the patches of sky visible through the thick tangle of half-bare branches and saw clouds sailing by.

Funny, he thought. *There's never any wind in Sleepy Hollow.*

Sam plugged in his iPod and skipped the first song — Bach's Partita in D Major. The blue Mustang was parked on the street. The old lady sat in her rocking chair at number two. Nothing stirred at number five. He wondered who lived in the other houses. He'd never seen anyone come or go from any of them.

There's something definitely wrong with this place, he decided.

Sam dribbled the ball. The *thunk, thunk, thunk* seemed to echo around him. He eyed the faded, rotting backboard, and worried that one good shot might bring the whole thing crashing down.

Squaring his shoulders to the basket, he bent his knees and jumped. As his feet left the asphalt, his elbow rose, his wrist flicked, and the ball glided off his fingertips. There was a lull in the music.

"The guy who used to live there really liked basketball."

Sam came down hard, nearly rolling his ankle. The ball hit the rim and flew back at him, hitting him in the arm and bouncing to the end of the driveway. He swung around yanking the iPod out of his ears.

Walter. Great, just what I need.

"I thought I told you not to sneak up on me," Sam snapped.

Walter was standing at the end of Sam's driveway. He picked up the ball. He wore the same pleated pants, cardigan, and mock turtleneck he always did. Only this time Sam noticed a dark stain across the collar.

Man, this is one dude in serious need of a makeover. And probably a shower.

Walter continued talking. "He'd play all the time. It was his favourite sport. He wasn't very good at it, though."

Sam rolled his eyes. It was as if the weirdo lived in his own little world. "Didn't you hear me? I said stop sneaking up on me." Sam held out his hands, but Walter clung to the ball. He was looking at it as if he hadn't seen one in years.

"Gimme the ball!" Sam demanded.

Walter ignored him and began dribbling the ball like a third-grader. He took a shot. It missed the rim by a mile, hit the garage door, and bounced down the driveway. Walter didn't even try to stop it. He just watched it roll past him and into the street.

Sam scowled. "Thanks a lot."

Walter stared at him, then smiled.

Sam shook his head. He brushed past Walter on his way to get the ball. It was resting against the curb in front of number two.

The old lady rocked back and forth, gazing vacantly like a zombie. At first Sam wasn't going to say anything, but then he thought he should try to act normal.

"Nice day," he mumbled, nearing her house.

He wasn't sure if she'd heard him, since she didn't reply. But then, as he was about to repeat himself, she croaked, "What's so nice about it?"

Sam was taken aback. Old ladies were supposed to be sweet. "Uh, well, I don't …" He wished he hadn't started the conversation. "Nice weather, I guess. Trees look nice."

"And how would I know about that? Can't see a thing. Blind as a bat."

She's blind? That's it. That's why she always stares into space.

Sam bent and picked up his ball. He almost dropped it. It was ice-cold, as if it had been locked inside a meat freezer. He glanced over to where Walter was, but the creep had already left.

"Oh ... uh ... sorry." Sam turned to walk back to his house.

"What are *you* sorry about?" the old lady demanded.

"Huh?"

"You deaf, boy? I asked you what you're so sorry about."

Sam's heart beat a little quicker. He'd read somewhere that people who were visually impaired developed acute hearing. Could she hear the *guilt* in his voice?

"N-nothing, I guess," he said, straining to sound calm and polite.

"Then stop walking around and apologizing for things you got nothing to do with," she growled.

Now Sam really wished he could end the conversation. "I gotta go."

"Have you heard the news?" she asked, ignoring his last comment.

News? Sam nearly buckled. Was the accident on the news? He should have checked the newspaper or the TV. "What *news?*" He tried to sound disinterested.

"Well, the *news*, of course," she snapped. "It's Hecate. She's moving back to Sleepy Hollow."

Sam took a deep breath. He was relieved — confused but relieved. *"Heck-ah-who?"* he asked.

"Hecate, you fool. She's coming home. After more than thirty years, she's coming home. It's about time, too. We haven't had one here in a while."

Sam had no idea what the old woman was squawking about, and frankly, he couldn't have cared less. Being visually impaired was obviously not the woman's only problem. Senility must be top of the list. Senile *and* rude.

"One?" he asked casually. "One what?"

"Witch, of course. Stupid boy. What else?"

A witch? More talk of *witches?* He couldn't deal with this. No way. Not today. Not on top of everything else.

"That's great, really," he said, turning again to leave. "Well, nice talking to you."

"Yes, you certainly do a lot of *talking*."

Sam stopped. Something about that last statement rubbed him the wrong way. He was finished with politeness. "And what's *that* supposed to mean?"

"Not much." She smiled. "Just that you were talking to yourself over there a while ago."

"Myself?" Sam was incensed. She might be senile, but *he* certainly wasn't. "I was not. I was talking to ..."

"Look, boy, I might be blind, but I sure ain't deaf. You were talking to yourself all right."

Sam narrowed his eyes and gritted his teeth. There was no point in arguing with a hundred-year-old nutcase who believed in witches.

CHAPTER NINETEEN

Sam tried all three news channels, but not one mentioned anything about the accident, not even the local station. He skimmed the newspaper, but there wasn't anything in there, either. Sam was about to head upstairs to check the minute-by-minute news blog when the door flew open. He could hear his parents arguing in hushed voices.

"Will you just leave me alone," his father said.

"I know the doctor says you're fine," his mother said, "but look at you, honey. Something's eating away at you. Why don't you tell me what it is?"

"Leave … me … *alone*!" his father snarled, slamming the front door behind him.

Sam cringed. His father was losing it. He never spoke that way to anyone, least of all his mother. Sam snuck a peek around the corner. His father was worse than ever. He was wearing a wool sweater, a scarf, a toque, and gloves as if it were the middle of winter! His eyes were dark and sunken. His skin was pale and drawn. How could the doctor say he was *fine*?

"It's this house," his mother whispered. "There's something dark in this house. I don't know how else to describe it. Ever since we moved in you haven't been yourself. You're always freezing. And you're on edge. Let's just get out of here, Robert."

"Move? Are you out of your mind?"

"Why not?" his mother asked. "We got it for a song. We can flip it and make money."

Leave Sleepy Hollow? Perfect idea, thought Sam. *Go back to Toronto. Leave the accident behind. Forget all about last night. About Cody and Ju —*

"This house was a dream come true," his father said. "It's a mansion, a real mansion, and you want to go back to that little dump in the city?" His tone was dark and menacing.

Sam's mother moved in closer, practically whispering in his father's ear. Sam leaned into the hall, trying to make out what she was saying.

"I haven't told you this before, Robert, but something about this place really gives me the creeps. I don't know exactly what it is, but it feels ... well ... like we're not *alone* in here." She eyed the ceiling and the walls, then caught sight of Sam lurking around the corner.

Sam took a step out of the family room as if he had just arrived. His mother smiled weakly. "Oh, hi, Sam." She fidgeted with her sleeves. "How was your morning?

Did Mike's dad pick him up all right?"

"Yeah." Sam shifted his gaze between his parents. "I was just heading upstairs to —"

"I'm glad Mike came up this weekend," his father said. "He's a good guy. You've stopped hanging around with that Barns boy, haven't you?"

"What? No. I mean, yes. I mean ..." Sam's cheeks got hotter.

"Oh, Robert, let him have his friends. You know how he has trouble making friends."

Sam's blood boiled. *Here we go again.* He moved quickly past them and headed upstairs, letting the new argument fade behind him. When he reached the door to his bedroom, he stopped short. The door was shut, but he could hear movement inside. *Tap, tap, tap,* as if someone were using his —

"Miranda!" he shouted, throwing the door open. It hit the wall with a whack and bounced back at him. He pushed it again and entered.

His sister was sitting at his desk. When she saw her brother, her eyes flashed with shock and embarrassment. She shut down the laptop with lightning speed. "You scared me half to death, you dummy!"

"Get out of my room, Miranda!" He eyed her suspiciously as she scrambled to her feet. "And why are you using *my* computer, anyway?"

"Mine froze up on me," she said quickly, "and Mom and Dad's has a password, and I needed to do … something …"

As she scurried past him, Sam glowered at her. "Stay out of my room, *Moronda*, or I swear, I'll —" He didn't finish his threat, since she was already halfway down the stairs.

Sam took a deep breath. His parents were getting on his case. His sister was bugging him. He was almost starting to feel normal again.

Sitting at his desk, he restarted his laptop. Still fuming, he began searching several news blogs but couldn't find a word about any car crash or fatality involving a person fitting Javon's description.

Wouldn't it be all over the news? Sam imagined the headline: LOCAL BOY DIES UNDER MYSTERIOUS CIRCUMSTANCES. Mysteries were always big in the news. After all, there was no impact to the vehicle. How would Javon have gotten from inside the car to underneath it? There had to be a write-up about the incident somewhere … unless … maybe Javon's family was blocking the story. Could they do that? Sam was puzzled.

Just then his cellphone began to vibrate. He'd forgotten all about his phone. The jeans he was wearing the previous night were on top of a pile of clothes on the floor. He lunged for them and dug the cell out of the pocket. He was sure it was Mike, but when he checked the call display, it read "Unknown Caller."

Sam flipped the phone open. "Yeah ..." he said tentatively.

At first there was no answer, just empty space.

"Hello?" he tried again. "Anyone there?"

Then he heard a voice, but it was choppy, as if the call was coming from another cell inside a building, an elevator, or an underground parking lot.

"Cody, is that you?"

Silence.

"Cody?"

The call dropped. The line was dead.

The phone buzzed again. He stared at it, refusing to answer. Finally, the buzzing stopped, but when he picked up the cell, it said he had one text message. He clicked and two words took shape on his screen: "Check blog."

Check blog? What blog?

Sam dropped the phone onto his desk. He had an idea, and clicked feverishly until Cody's blog appeared on the screen with its familiar frothy-jowled Doberman. There were no new entries. The last one still read:

> Maestro learns how to stunt ... detes to follow ...

> Posted: September 7, 10:30 p.m.

Only now Sam saw that instead of two comments posted, there were five. He clicked on them. The first comment had been from Homegirl, the second from Javon. When Sam read Javon's name, a shiver crept up his spine. He quickly scanned the next comment. It was another from Homegirl:

> So, Maniac, is there one more fool in this world or what?
>
> Posted: September 9, 11:30 p.m.

Cody responded:

> Nah, nothing new to report.
>
> Posted: September 9, 11:35 p.m.

Sam clenched his teeth. *What a liar!* It was as if the guy had no conscience whatsoever. A stone-cold liar. A sociopath capable of anything.

There was one more comment. Sam's eyes focused on it. He sat still for the longest time, not blinking, not breathing. The message read:

I know what you did last night. I know what happened.

Posted: September 9, 00:00 a.m.

The message was signed "Anonymous."

Sam's jaw muscles went limp, and his breath caught somewhere in his chest. Then, suddenly, a frantic urge overcame him. He forced control over his limbs and started clicking furiously, opening his email account and hitting the send/receive button. There were eleven new messages. One by one they appeared in his inbox. He felt the blood drain slowly from his body.

≣ Unknown [Bulk] Re: I know what you did!
≣ Unknown [Bulk] Re: I know what you did!
≣ Unknown [Bulk] Re: I know what you did!
≣ Unknown [Bulk] Re: I know what you did!
≣ Unknown [Bulk] Re: I know what you did!
≣ Unknown [Bulk] Re: I know what you did!
≣ Unknown [Bulk] Re: I know what you did!
≣ Unknown [Bulk] Re: I know what you did!
≣ Unknown [Bulk] Re: I know what you did!
≣ Unknown [Bulk] Re: I know what you did!
≣ Unknown [Bulk] Re: I know what you did!

CHAPTER TWENTY

Sam leaned his head against the window of the school bus as it sped down the Tenth Line. He couldn't bear the thought of passing the spot where he and Cody had left Javon, so he was sitting on the opposite side of the bus with his eyes shut. Sam hadn't slept in two nights. His head throbbed and his mind was soupy. He was nearly drifting asleep when the bus hit a large pothole and bounced him awake. Instinctively, he scanned the street.

It was the exact spot.

Sam shuddered, and his stomach lurched. Bitter bile rose at the back of his throat. He fought hard to swallow it. Then his eyes met Walter's. The creep was sitting five rows up — alone as usual. He had his head turned practically all the way around and was smiling his freaky smile.

Could it be him? Sam wondered. *Did Walter send the cryptic message?* Sam knew all too well how Walter could skulk around practically unnoticed. Sometimes he even felt as if Walter was following him — everywhere. *Did Walter see me leaving the house Saturday night? Did he follow me and see me getting into the car with Cody and Javon? Did he know about Cody's blog? Does he know about the accident?*

Thoughts whirled inside Sam's mind as the bus hit the brakes, the door flung open, and Cody got on. Swaggering down the aisle to the back of the bus as if it was just another ordinary day, as though he didn't have a care in the world, he threw himself into the seat beside Sam. AJ got on behind Cody; only this time she sat at the front of the bus.

"What are you doing?" Sam whispered through clenched teeth. "You're supposed to stay away from me. And what's with AJ? Why's she sitting up there?"

Cody grinned. "Chill, Maestro."

Sam wanted to knock out the guy's teeth. How could he act this way when they'd just killed his best friend? Sam was having a hard time breathing, and here was Cody all smug and stupid smiles.

Has the whole world gone insane? Sam wondered. *Or is it just me?*

"Does AJ know? Did you tell her?"

"No way, man. She doesn't know a thing. We just had a fight, is all. You know how girls are. Everything's cool. No one knows anything."

"Oh, yeah?" Sam said. "Check your blog lately?" He fixed Cody with a withering glare. "Someone *knows*."

The grin slid from Cody's lips. "No way. I thought that was *you*, man."

Sam lost it. "Why would I write something like that, you idiot!"

"Whoa!" Cody scanned the other riders. "Keep your voice down. Act normal. Stop attracting attention."

Act normal? Normal? Nothing will ever be normal again.

"Well, it wasn't me," Sam whispered. "So, *genius*, that means someone else knows. We are *so* going down for this — and it's all *your* fault. We should have stayed. We should have called the cops right then and there ... told them it was an accident ... told them the truth."

"Relax. There's no proof of anything. Nothing to link us to the accident."

"No, of course not," Sam said. "Nothing at all, except maybe *forensics*, you moron!"

"Will you kill the insults, dude. We're in this *together*, remember?"

How could Sam forget? For the first time he found himself wishing he'd listened to his father and stayed away from Cody. His dad had said that all Ringwood Barnses were no good — how did he know?

"Listen, what's done is done," Cody said. "Just stay

cool and we'll ride this out. They must think it's an accident, anyway."

"What makes you so sure?"

"No 5-0, Maestro." Cody was smiling again. "Cops would've called me for sure."

Cody had a point. But that didn't make sense. Why wouldn't the police call Cody, even just to see if he knew anything? Maybe the police were toying with them. Maybe they already knew everything. Maybe they had Cody and him under surveillance. Maybe the police were waiting for the right moment. Maybe they were secretly videoing them and hoping to catch them saying something incriminating ...

Stop it! Sam ordered himself. *Now you're sounding totally paranoid.*

He took a deep breath as the bus halted in front of the elementary school and Miranda exited. She looked back over her shoulder at Sam and grinned.

Sam started wondering about his sister. Miranda had been in his room using his computer. Possibly tracking his Internet moves? Perhaps sending messages? It was possible that she heard him leave the house on Saturday. Then again, it could be Mike. Maybe Mike hadn't left the roadside. Maybe he'd been hiding there. Maybe he'd seen something. Heard something ...

Enough! Sam's mind screamed. *Ridiculous!* Mike

had been home. In his room. He didn't know anything. He couldn't know. Sam scrunched his eyes, took a deep breath, and tried to clear his head, but visions of legs sticking out from under cars, bikes rolling down hills, cars colliding, and bloody, headless bodies swam in the endless black waters of his conscience.

"Did you get rid of those pictures and the video clip I sent you?" Sam asked Cody, suddenly remembering the photos he'd taken that night.

"Video?" Cody narrowed his eyes. "No, man. No video. You sent me two pictures. That's it. One of the top of my head and one of a pair of feet. You're a crappy photographer, man."

Sam sat bolt upright and searched his memory. Two pictures and a video. He'd sent all three to Cody. He was absolutely certain. And the video had all the incriminating evidence. "I sent you two pictures and a video."

"No way. Uh-uh." Cody shook his head. "I only got the pictures."

"I sent you a video!" Sam insisted. "I remember exactly. I took two pictures and one video. Each time I hit the options key, scrolled down, and ... and sent them off."

"So tell me then, Maestro, if I got the two pictures, who got the video?"

The bus pulled up to the school. A squad car was parked in front of the principal's office.

CHAPTER TWENTY-ONE

Cate Wolfe arched her thin eyebrows. "Poor Ichabod."
She walked to the front of her desk, sat on the edge, and
crossed her long legs.

Sam sank low in his chair. *His homework!* He hadn't
finished it. He hadn't read the end of the story, hadn't
done the one-page summary. Ms. Wolfe might be young
and pretty, but she was a drill sergeant. Sam knew he was
going to catch it, but somehow, given all that was happening, it was the least of his worries.

"When last we left Ichabod Crane, visions of the
plump and pretty Katrina Van Tassel danced in his brain.
He was invited to a party at the Van Tassel home. So
what went wrong?"

An enthusiastic hand shot up in the front row. "Well,
on his way home from the party, Ichabod let his fears
get the better of him," said a perky voice that belonged
to the hand. "And Brom Bones, who wanted Katrina all
to himself, scared Ichabod off by pretending to be the
Headless Horseman."

"Okay." Ms. Wolfe smiled as if she knew something the class didn't. "That's one take on the story. Let's look at this passage." She read:

> On mounting a rising ground, which brought
> the figure of his fellow-traveller in relief
> against the sky, gigantic in height, and muf-
> fled in a cloak, Ichabod was horror-struck, on
> perceiving that he was headless!

"Now," continued the teacher, "who thinks good ol' Ichabod got punked by Brom Bones?"

Laughter erupted, and several hands waved.

"And who thinks he was murdered by the Headless Horseman?"

Headless ... headless ... headless ...

The word reverberated in Sam's mind. The room dimmed, then brightened, then dimmed again. Every breath he took was a struggle. It was as if he were drowning and no matter how hard he inhaled there wasn't enough air to fill his lungs. He rubbed his eyes. They felt scratchy and sore. Visions of the bloody stump atop the body in the front seat of the car twisted in his brain. There had been something eerily familiar about the woman and that body. *What was it?*

Sam ran a hand through his hair and yawned. Ms. Wolfe was talking, but he wasn't listening. All he could think about was Javon and that strange vision he'd had. Riding the bike, the accident, the blood — all that blood. It had been a hallucination he told himself, and yet, why had everything seemed so real, so incredibly familiar?

"Take out your assignment," Ms. Wolfe said, returning to her desk. "Bring it to me when I call your name."

Sam glanced at Cody. There was nothing on his desk. *Figures,* he thought. *Cody's a loser. Just like Dad said. How did he know?*

"Detention," Ms. Wolfe said when Cody showed up at her desk empty-handed. "Detention," she repeated when Sam arrived likewise. "And be prepared to stay until your summary is complete. I've got all the time in the world …"

───────────

Sam called his house, but when his father answered, he pressed end. His dad would be furious with him for getting a detention. He'd call back once he'd figured out something else to tell him.

The rest of the day swirled by like a dream. Sam walked from class to class like a robot, though he did manage to keep a sleepy eye out for the police.

At lunch he sat alone. Cody and AJ were in a heated discussion at another table. He didn't care. Sam was too tired and too dazed to care about anyone or anything anymore. He took a sip of his pop and stared blankly at his uneaten fries.

Something was wrong. Why wasn't there any sort of memorial for Javon? Why was no one talking about his death? Something like this usually brought an entire community, let alone a high school, to a complete stand-still. And yet here at Ringwood Secondary it was business as usual.

Nothing made any sense.

Sam wondered again if he was under surveillance. *Are the police keeping a tight lid on the information until they can pin it on someone?* Out of the corner of his eye Sam studied everyone and everything he passed with a mistrusting scowl.

By the end of the school day, Sam was so exhausted that he felt dizzy. He couldn't remember the last time he'd slept. It was all he could do to keep himself upright. Sam called his house again, and when the voice mail picked up, he left a message, saying he was staying for extra help. He figured that would appease his parents. Then he headed to his English room.

"Welcome," Cate Wolfe said as Sam entered. "Take a seat and get to work. Sooner your assignment's done, sooner you leave."

"Do you, uh, have an extra copy of the story?" he asked.

Ms. Wolfe frowned, then reached into her desk drawer and pulled out a spare. She handed it to Sam just as Cody sauntered into the room.

Sam ignored him and sat at the opposite end of the room by the window. He had to read the rest of the story before he could do the summary, but each time he tried the words blurred and his head pounded. Sam snatched bits and pieces as the ink swam around on the page:

> ... opening in the trees ... reach that bridge
> ... I am safe ... safe ... reach that bridge ...
> convulsive kick ... pursuer ... hurling his head
> ... his head ... head ... tremendous crash ...
> black steed ... goblin ... whirlwind ...

Taking a deep breath, Sam tossed the pages aside. Ms. Wolfe looked up briefly, narrowed her eyes, then went back to grading papers.

Sam sat for the longest time, unable to form a clear thought. He kept eyeing the clock as seconds turned into minutes and minutes slipped away. Sam needed to get out of the class, needed to get home and get some sleep. He put pen to paper and wrote:

> Ichabod Crane was a geeky teacher who moved to a weird place called Sleepy Hollow. He was a greedy kind of guy, and when he

found out this girl named Katrina was single and rich, he wanted to marry her. But other guys, like this one named Brom Bones, liked Katrina, too.

One day Ichabod got invited to a party. He danced a bit with Katrina and then things went bad. He left the party, and while riding home, he got attacked by the Headless Horseman and disappeared. He was never seen again.

There, he thought. *Done. That's all she's going to get out of me.*

Sam picked up the story and his assignment and strode to the teacher's desk. He held his assignment out for her to see. She glanced at the paper and frowned. For a second Sam thought she was going to make him rewrite the assignment, but then she accepted his paper and placed it on her pile of work. Sam was about to leave when she cleared her throat.

"So, Mr. McLean, did you find some old-timer with nothing better to do than to spin yarns about Sleepy Hollow?"

"Maybe. Sort of." *If you could count a senile old-timer.*

"Well, *I* did," Ms. Wolfe said.

For the first time that day a surge of energy zipped through Sam's veins. He perked up and focused. "Really?"

"I heard that the houses in Sleepy Hollow are over a hundred years old, but that the community itself is much older than that."

Sam watched her eyes grow wider as she spoke until they were two black glistening pools. There was something mesmerizing about them. Something mesmerizing about her.

"Sleepy Hollow was once a collection of frame houses dating back to the earliest settlers in the region."

Sam nodded. *Okay. It's old. I get the picture.*

She leaned in closer, her voice dropping to a whisper. "Some say those settlers, the ones that built Sleepy Hollow, they were all *witches.*" Her lips lingered for a moment on that last word. "A coven of witches who moved up north from New England. Came here to escape persecution."

Sam's mouth went dry. He tried to swallow but couldn't muster enough saliva. *A coven of witches? The old lady was right!*

"One of the more modern legends spoke of a witch who was killed in an accident years ago. They say that with her dying breath she cursed the place — those responsible for her accident *and* their descendants." The teacher leaned back in her chair. Her voice and tone returned to normal. "That's all I found out. Kind of creepy, eh?" She smiled and batted her eyes, stared at him a moment longer, then resumed marking the papers.

Sam was unable to move. This was nuts. Trashy gossip. *There's no such thing as a witch*, he told himself.

He glanced over at Cody. The guy's head was bent. He was scratching something onto his paper, apparently oblivious to the conversation. Sam looked back at Ms. Wolfe. She glanced up at him again and smiled.

The whole town was nuts!

Sam had the sudden urge to leave. Get away. Get out of the class. Out of the school. Out of Ringwood and out of Sleepy Hollow.

He darted from the room and raced down the hall. It was almost four-thirty. The school was nearly empty except for a few stragglers hanging around their lockers. Sam's head pounded. He felt as if the entire world were spinning around him.

Stupid. Ridiculous. There's no such thing as a witch ...

Sam stopped in front of his locker, opened it, and reached inside to grab his backpack. He yanked it out and heard something tear. Sam was about to slam his locker door when something fluttered to the ground. It was a torn piece of paper with a note scrawled on it.

Sam picked up the torn slip of paper and held it in trembling hands. His eyes flew over the words etched in jagged letters:

I know the truth.
I know what really happened.

Sam's knees wobbled and nearly gave out. He fell back against the row of lockers. The world was spinning again.

Who was after him? Who knew the truth? He quickly scanned the halls, but none of the stragglers seemed to be paying him any attention. One kid was tying his shoelace. Two girls were giggling near the doors to the gym. Then, suddenly, he caught sight of a figure as it darted around the corner at the far end of the hall.

It was Walter. Sam was sure of it. He'd know that frizzy black hair anywhere.

He's gone too far. He's not going to get away with this!

Sam crumpled the note in his fist. His knuckles were white. He'd show Walter. He'd ram the paper down his throat and make him eat his words.

Leaving his locker wide open and letting his backpack drop to the ground, Sam tore down the hall. He nearly ran into the guy who was tying his shoelace but sidestepped him at the last second.

"Watch it!" the guy shouted.

But Sam just kept running.

He spun past the girls, who stopped giggling. He ignored their gasps and charged forward, reaching the end of the hall in a matter of seconds. He took the corner too fast, swung wide, and almost slammed into the wall on the opposite side.

"Walter!" Sam roared at the top of his lungs.

He didn't care that he was at school, didn't care what might happen to him if he got caught shrieking in the hallway. All he cared about at that moment was grabbing Walter by the throat and choking that smug smile off of his face once and for all. But before Sam could finish his thought, he came to an abrupt standstill.

The hall was empty. The figure — whoever it was — was gone.

Sam kicked wildly at a locker door, slamming his foot into it so hard that he dented the metal. He dropped to the ground, cursing and grabbing his foot. Squeezing his eyes shut, he swallowed the throbbing pain, trying desperately to get hold of himself. He was furious, frustrated, exhausted, and confused. Part of him wanted to lie on the floor for the rest of eternity, while the other part wanted to put his fist through a wall. He took a deep breath, exhaled slowly through clenched teeth, and opened his eyes.

The principal, Mr. Gordon, was standing three feet away, staring down at Sam. The short, bald man scowled, then motioned calmly for Sam to follow him.

Sam sighed. Things couldn't possibly get any worse. He scooped up the crumpled ball of paper he'd dropped and shoved it into his back pocket.

———————

"Robert McLean," the principal said when Sam's father entered the office a half-hour later.

Sam glanced up from the chair he'd been slumped in, and for the first time in his life he was ashamed of his father. Totally ashamed.

His dad was wearing three layers of clothing that looked as if he'd slept in them. He was unshaven. It seemed as if he hadn't had a shower in days. His face was starting to show what appeared to be some sort of weird disease — all white and blotchy, with dark greenish rings around bloodshot eyes.

This wasn't his father. Someone had kidnapped Mr. Perfect and left Zombie Dude behind.

"Norm," his father said, nodding in acknowledgement.

Sam's spine straightened. His father *knew* the principal? He actually *knew* him? Somehow Sam had forgotten that his father had grown up in Ringwood, that he likely knew a lot of the people.

"Surprised to see you here, Bobby," the principal said, eyeing Sam's father with a mixture of amusement and contempt. "Thought you'd left Ringwood for good."

Bobby? No one calls Dad Bobby.

"What's this all about, Norm?"

Sam studied his father's expression. It was stone-cold, almost sinister. Sam knew right then and there he could kiss his iPod goodbye. And his computer. And his cellphone.

Almost out of reflex Sam gazed out the window of the office. The sun was low in the sky. A golden haze bathed the football field. In the opposite direction, darkness brewed. A storm approached in silence.

"Your son went berserk, Bobby. Kicked in a locker and was cussing at the top of his lungs. Thing is, there wasn't anyone else around."

Sam was waiting for his father to look over and shake his head, roll his eyes, do something to demonstrate disappointment, but he didn't cast him even a sideways glance. Instead, he kept his eyes trained on the principal, as though Sam wasn't even in the room.

"I'll pay to have the locker repaired," he said with a calmness that was frightening. "And you won't be hearing any foul language coming out of this boy's mouth again." He paused, then added, "*That's* a promise."

Sam swallowed a lump the size of a baseball. That was no promise. That was a warning.

The principal studied him for a moment as if he were taking great pleasure in deciding his fate. Finally, he said, "All right. I'll cut him some slack, Bobby. But keep a tight rein on your boy. I've seen him hanging round with Cody Barns. *You*, of all people, should know that can't come to any good. In fact, just today the police were here. That's all I can say."

Sam's eyes grew wide, and his pulse quickened. *The police. Cody. They must know. Everything.*

"Sam won't be seeing the Barns boy anymore," his father said, smiling. It was a thin grin, barely noticeable, but Sam caught it. Then he added, "That's another *promise*."

CHAPTER TWENTY-THREE

They walked to the station wagon without saying a word. Sam dragged two paces behind his father, steering clear of the firing zone. The air was thick. The storm was moving toward them quickly. Sam could taste it at the back of his throat.

The car ride was torture. Sam's father refused to look at him, let alone say a single word. Sam felt as if his head were on the chopping block and that at any second a razor-sharp axe was going to drop. He opened his mouth once to speak, but then thought better of it. Instead, he studied his father for a moment, then leaned back into the cool leather seat and closed his eyes.

As the car sped up the Tenth Line, Sam's mind drifted. *Bobby. No one ever calls Mr. Perfect Bobby. No one that doesn't have a death wish, that is.*

Something was worming its way through Sam's subconscious, struggling to free itself. *Bobby. That name. That person riding the bike ... the Kronan ...*

Sam opened his eyes. The Volvo was headed uphill.

They were at the spot where he'd last seen Javon, where he'd first seen the riderless bike.

He had so many things he wanted to say to his father that he didn't know where to start. "Dad," he began tentatively.

His father didn't respond. He merely stared out the windshield at the country road and beyond it.

Sam took a deep breath and tried again. "Dad?"

It was as if he wasn't there.

The third time Sam couldn't contain himself. The questions gushed out of his mouth as the dam he'd built in his mind burst. "Dad, remember that bike we saw coming down the hill? Do you remember it? Was it a *red* bike? An *old* bike? Did it have the word *Kronan* written on the crossbar? Did it look like something Grandpa would have ridden?"

Sam wasn't expecting what happened next. His father slammed a foot down so hard on the brakes that the car screeched to a sudden halt in the middle of the road. Luckily, Sam had his seat belt on or he'd have gone right through the windshield. His father threw the car into park and drilled Sam with bloodshot eyes. For a moment Sam didn't recognize his father. His face was distorted with something more than rage.

"Who told you about it?" His voice was deep and gravelly.

Sam was wide-eyed. *Who is this guy?*

His father leaned in closer. "Who told you?" Spittle gathered in the corners of his mouth.

Suddenly, Sam was reminded of the frothing Doberman on Cody's blog.

"I'm only going to ask you one more time, Sam," Robert said, trying to force calmness into his voice. The effect was opposite. It was like a quiet hysteria.

It's as if he's under some kind of evil spell ... a witch's spell! The witches of Sleepy Hollow!

"How do you know about the Kronan? Who told you? Was it that Barns boy? What lies has he been telling you about me?"

"I ... I don't know what you ... you mean, Dad," Sam stammered. Instinctively, he undid his seat belt and pressed his back against the passenger door.

The Tenth Line was dead. Darkness loomed. The headlights, beaming straight ahead, sliced through the gloom. Sam kept glancing up the road, hoping another car would approach and force his father's attention back to the road, snap him out of this spell, but none came.

"I know you know something, Sam. I see it in your eyes. Every time you look at me. I see it. You *know*. You know everything. Don't lie to me."

Lightning flashed, igniting a flame in his father's eyes that glowed long after the brightness had disappeared.

"I ... I really don't know what you mean, Dad. I ... I just wanted to know about the bike."

"That's it! That bike. How do you know about it?"

Thunder groaned.

"You know how I know about it." Sam tried to sound casual, but his heart pounded against his ribs like a jackhammer. He was scared and furious at the same time. What was his father accusing him of? Why didn't he trust him?

"I saw it, Dad. Don't you remember? We *both* saw it. Coming down the hill at us. Right here. The day we moved to this stupid place."

Sam's father scrunched his eyes and ran shaking hands through his hair as though he were thinking really hard about something. "Now this is the part I don't understand." His father stared through the windshield into the darkness. "The bike we saw coming down this hill was just a regular bike, Sam. One of those new bikes kids ride today. Not the *Kronan*. Who told you about the *Kronan*?" He pounded his fists into the steering wheel, and the horn blared.

"It's like I told you, Dad. I saw it here. *Right here*."

"You're a liar! I didn't bring you up to lie! I didn't raise you to kick in lockers or get into trouble at school or —"

"No, you raised me to be perfect — like *you*!" Sam had reached his limit. He couldn't hold himself back any longer. "Don't you know how hard it is to try to be perfect every second of every single day?" Tears welled in his eyes, and he felt his cheeks burn. "I'm sick of having to do everything you want me to do. I'm sick of having to be perfect. And I'm sick of you!"

Robert reached for Sam, but his seat belt yanked him back. Suddenly, Sam knew he had to get out, had to get away. He threw open the door and fled into the field toward a cluster of trees. Sam could hear his father yelling at him to get back into the car, but he kept running with long, gangly strides, stealing quick glances back as flashes of lightning lit up the Volvo and the figure of his father beside it.

Thunder rumbled again, this time louder and closer, and the clouds split open. As Sam raced through the mud and brush, drops of cold rain pelted his face. Tall grass slowed him, but he pushed himself harder, ducking into the woods and pressing against the trunk of a huge maple. His heart thudded against his ribs. His mind was a jumble of thoughts. What was he going to do? Where was he going to go?

Sam heard his father's voice rise over the storm. "Sam! Sam! Get back here! Sam!"

CHAPTER TWENTY-FOUR

Sam shut his eyes and swallowed great gulps of moist air. His father's screams started to fade behind the wall of pounding rain until finally they stopped altogether. Was his dad tracking him? Would he find him?

Slowly, Sam mustered enough courage to open his eyes and peer around the tree. Lightning flashed, and Sam stole a glimpse of the road.

It was empty. The Volvo was gone.

Like a marionette with its strings cut, Sam sank into a squatting position, his back against the tree trunk. Rain dripped through the dying foliage, bringing the odd leaf down along with it. What was he going to do? Who could he turn to?

Sam wrapped his arms tightly around his drenched body. Salty tears mingled with the rain that now streaked his face.

Mike, he thought. *I'll call Mike. He'll know.*

Shivering, Sam dug into the pocket of his jeans and found his cellphone. He flipped it open. The neon-blue light of the screen split the darkness. He scrolled through the *M*'s, passed Maniac, and found Mike. Sam was about to press call when the phone began to vibrate. Startled, he nearly dropped the cell. The call display read: "Unknown Caller."

"H-hello?" he attempted to say, but no sound came out. His throat had turned to chalk. He coughed and tried again, this time managing a whispered "H-hello?"

A loud crack of thunder blasted his ears and shook the ground beneath him. It rumbled for several seconds. When there was another flash of lightning, Sam thought he saw a headless figure crouched near a distant tree trunk, but then darkness swallowed the world again, leaving him believing it had been nothing more than a trick of the light bouncing off a rotting stump.

Sam pressed the phone to his ear, straining to hear even the faintest sound, but nothing came. He lifted it to his eyes and studied the screen. The call hadn't dropped. He was still connected ... to someone ... somewhere ...

"W-who is this?" he asked, trying desperately to force a semblance of courage into his voice.

Another few seconds passed before he heard something. The words were slow, stretched out like taffy. "Meet me ... at the old willow ... tonight ...

Sam's pulse raced, and his mind sprinted to keep up. *The old willow? Tonight?*

He wanted to say something, anything, but his voice had deserted him. Finally, he cleared his throat and sputtered, "Who ... who is this? What do you want from me?"

Silence.

Sam tried again, louder, more forceful, but it was no use. He checked the phone. The caller was gone.

His thigh muscles gave out, and he plunked himself onto the ground, letting the phone fall into his lap. He rubbed his face with trembling hands. Why was this happening to him? Why would someone want to meet him at the old willow? Why now in the middle of a storm?

At the same time Sam scanned his memory. That voice — there was something weird about it. Weird and ... familiar. Who was it? Was it his father? No. Sam shook his head, spraying drops of rain from his hair. Surely, he'd recognize his own father's voice.

Was it Walter? Was that creep still taunting him with stupid games? Was it Cody? Or was it ...? Could it be ...?

Sam's stomach lurched, and before he knew what was happening, he was on his knees, spewing his insides onto the damp earth and decomposing leaves. He coughed and spat several times until he regained control of his stomach and nerves. He took several long breaths, his fingers clawing the ground. Sam had nowhere to go and no one to turn to. He wanted to race back to the Tenth Line and head south, run away from home and never look back. He was a coward. A chicken. He hated himself.

The vault inside his brain, the one he'd kept locked for what seemed like forever, snapped open, and a river of unwanted memories gushed forth, nearly drowning him.

There was Sam picked last for every game. There was Sam standing alone in the playground, kids fleeing from him as if he had some kind of disease. Kids laughing at him. Teasing him. Calling him names. Looking at him with disgust in eyes that said: "You worthless piece of trash. You don't deserve to be treated any better." And the worst part of all, the saddest, most pathetic part, was that he, Sam, agreed with them. He had let them do it because deep down he believed they were right.

Sam hung his head. He was so disappointed. He thought he'd escaped that person. He thought if he wore the mask long enough it would fuse to his face and become him. But, no, he hadn't changed. He hadn't stood up to Cody. He should never have gone with him in the first place. And when everything had gotten out of control, he hadn't done what his instincts had told him to do. He should have stayed and called the police.

You haven't changed, he told himself. *You're that same stupid kid. You want Mike to save you, like always.*

"No," he whispered to himself, making a fist and pressing it into his thigh. The incessant rain drowned out his voice. "No!" he cried a second time, this time slamming his fist so hard into the fleshy part of his leg that he knew there would be a purple mark there the next day.

Sam spat and dragged a sleeve across his mouth. He picked up the phone that had fallen into the dirt, shoved it into his pocket, rose on trembling legs, and studied the darkness. Beyond the wooded area the rain was a thick grey curtain lit by flashes of lightning. Sam braced himself. He had a long walk home, but there was no turning back now. He'd have to face the ghosts of his past sooner or later. And his father. And whoever was sending him the messages.

"All right," he said, tilting his chin upward, "let's see who you are."

CHAPTER TWENTY-FIVE

Sam slogged through the muck, heading toward the Tenth Line. He had to face this whole thing down — whatever it was — or it would haunt him forever. When he reached the road, he stopped briefly at the spot where he'd last seen Javon, where he'd last seen his father. Taking a deep breath, Sam forced both images from his mind and kept walking, hiking north along the shoulder of the road. It was the second time in less than a week that he found himself making this long trek. The first time he'd been running from something. This time he was moving steadily toward it.

Ever since he'd moved to Sleepy Hollow, Sam had felt as though something had been stalking him. Whichever way he turned, whichever way he moved, there was something not quite there, fluttering around him, following him, clinging to him like a foul stench. This night was no different. He kept his eyes and ears open.

The sky was a box of steel wool. The rain had let up. Drops no longer blasted his face but buzzed past him like a swarm of tiny insects. The lightning and thunder were behind him now, distant, less threatening.

More than once Sam resisted the urge to call Mike. Cold seeped through his skin and flesh, right into his very bones. He moved with slow, steady strides, his brain stuck on one thought: *This all ends tonight.*

Even for the usually quiet Tenth Line the road seemed strangely deserted. After almost two kilometres, not one single car had passed Sam in either direction. He had cleared the hilly area and was now in the straightaway, less than a kilometre from the old weeping willow that stood guard beside the entrance to Sleepy Hollow.

Sam checked his cell. It was almost 8:00 p.m. Sam wondered what state his father was in, if he'd calmed down yet, but decided not to think about him yet. He knew his mother was probably worried sick. What had his father told her? Had they called the police, or did they figure he'd have no choice but to come home eventually?

"Home," he muttered softly to himself. The word stuck in Sam's throat like someone else's chewed-up gum. It had been ten days since they had moved into the old house, and it felt less like home now than it had that first night. How he wished they had never left his old house in Toronto, and yet, somehow, with each step he took along the gravelly shoulder of the desolate road, he sensed more and more that he was meant to come here, to Ringwood, to Sleepy Hollow, that this was all somehow meant to happen.

Sam had felt his entire life as if he were standing on the brink of a dark pit — an endless chasm. *Don't move! Don't breathe!* One wrong step, one false move, and he'd plunge into darkness for eternity. Fear had him paralyzed.

Now, for the first time, he had a new thought, a simple notion. Why hadn't it come to him before? *Step back,* he told himself. *Just step back and walk away.*

Tonight that was what he would do. He'd take a step back, face the past, fix it, and then move on in a totally new direction. Simple.

When Sam reached the old willow, he stopped. He stood for a moment, studying the graceful crown of branches that swept the ground. The enormous trunk was grey and cut deep with fissures. For the first time he noticed the tree was twisted — three separate trunks winding around one another to form a single massive trunk. There was something majestic about this tree, he thought, majestic and at the same time eerie. Wind and drizzle flew through the air, and Sam thought he heard an eerie melody whispering through the half-bare branches.

"This tree must be two hundred years old," he mumbled to himself.

"Older," said a voice that Sam at first didn't recognize.

Sam watched as the dark figure peered out of the tangle of branches. Those hooded eyes, that sheepish grin — this wasn't who he was expecting.

"What do you want from me, man?" Sam demanded, taking a step toward the figure. Even in the faint sliver of moon that now peeked through the black clouds, Sam recognized confusion seep into Cody's eyes.

"You tripping or what? You're the one who wanted to meet here, Maestro. I should be asking you the same question."

Sam took another step closer. "You called *me*. You asked *me* to meet *you* here. What's going on?"

Cody also moved forward. The two were now standing face to face. "I didn't call you, man. I thought you called me. Someone did. They said: 'Meet me at the old willow tonight.' If it wasn't you, then who was it? Who wanted us both here?"

Sam knew the answer. It was him. The blackmailer — Walter. Instinctively, Sam scanned the forest. Walter was out there somewhere, waiting, watching.

"Walter!" he called, his voice thick and hollow. "We know you're out there, so you might as well show yourself."

There was a rustling in the leaves to Sam's right. Someone was definitely there. He'd bet his life on it.

"Walter?" Cody looked more puzzled than ever. "Who's that?"

"You've seen him on the bus. Geeky. Old-fashioned clothes. Wears the same stuff all the time."

Cody shrugged. "No idea who you're talking about, Maestro. Never heard of any Walter."

Sam shook his head and rolled his eyes. Of course, he hadn't. Why would he? Walter and Maniac couldn't be farther apart on the similarity scale. A guy like Walter would be invisible to someone like Cody.

"Walter!" Sam called again. "I know it's you. Just come out and tell us what you want."

There was movement in the trees. A rustling of branches and dead leaves. Soft steps on soggy ground. Someone was coming closer.

CHAPTER TWENTY-SIX

It was still drizzling, but Sam no longer noticed the rain. He held his breath, hoping to steady his racing pulse. His legs had grown roots and were planted firmly on the ground. Each second lasted an hour. The rustling drew nearer.

Why are you so scared? he asked himself. *It's only Walter and you can take him with one hand tied behind your back. What are you so afraid of?*

Sam shook his head. He remembered he was no longer going to sit around and let life happen to him. He was in control. He was in the driver's seat. And suddenly he found energy in his legs and began moving step by step toward the noise until he disappeared under the canopy of intertwining branches.

"Hey!" Cody shouted. "Where are you going, dude?"

But Sam ignored him. He was on a mission. He'd show Walter once and for all who was boss.

The forest was deep and dark. Sam could barely see his hand in front of his face. He listened for the snapping of twigs. Movement to his right. No … his left. Sam picked up the pace, slashing through the tangle of branches, moving as quickly as his legs would allow. Needles scraped against his exposed flesh as he scrambled toward the sound that seemed to lead him deeper and deeper into the forest.

This is crazy! he told himself. *These woods aren't that deep. I should be coming out into the houses soon. Where are the houses?*

Sam's lungs felt as if they were filling up with sand. He gasped for air, sputtered, and coughed, all the while flying toward the noise that seemed to move in one direction, then another, coming from in front of him, behind him, all around him.

"Walter!" he shouted, his voice heavy and dull.

Then he saw it. Saw *him*. A figure draped in shadows. A figure standing straight and tall. A figure with no *head*!

Sam shuddered. He blinked hard, but the figure was still there. A shape of shoulders, of spidery limbs. A human shape with nothing but a ragged, jagged stump where there should have been a head!

Impossible, he thought. *This is so not real!*

Sam mustered all the courage he could. "What … who are you?"

There was no reply. He repeated the question. Still no response.

And then there was a low grow, a rumbling from deep in the earth, and something spewed out of the jagged stump where there should have been a head. Thick and dark liquid sprayed into the air as though the figure were a grotesque fountain, sprinkling Sam's face, oozing onto the ground, flowing all around him, dripping from the trees. *Blood! It was blood! Everywhere!* Sam could taste it as it dripped like rain down his nose and cheeks and into his mouth. It was blood — there was no doubt about it.

Run! Sam's brain commanded his legs. *Run!*

With every once of strength in him, Sam scrambled backward through the thick woods toward the spot where he'd left Cody. Panic seized his throat and squeezed. He couldn't breathe. A searing pain forced his hand to his side, but he couldn't stop. It was coming. Whatever it was, it was after him. He could hear it. Smell it. Taste it.

The dream! he remembered suddenly. *My dream!* Only now Sam had the very real sense that if he didn't outrun whatever was after him, he'd never live to wake up again.

One linc from the old legend echoed in his brain like music on a scratched CD: *Ichabod was spirited away by supernatural means ... spirited away ... spirited away ...*

Sam hurtled through the woods, darting this way, then that, spinning crazily out of control. He nearly fell several times, but managed to snatch his balance back at the last second. Whatever it was, it was gaining on him. He could hear it close behind, felt an icy wind prickle the back of his neck. He didn't want to be spirited away!

"Got ... to get ... out of here ..." he gasped.

Sam had lost all sense of time. How long had he been running? How much farther was it? The willow tree was just ahead. He'd make it to the clearing. He'd make it, he told himself.

A wheezing grew loud in Sam's ears. It was right behind him. And then, just as he broke through the veil of branches, his body flew forward face first into the damp earth, twigs, and stones. It had caught him! Tackled him! It was on top of him, its weight pressing against him, clawing at him to turn him over. He squeezed his eyes shut and screamed as the monster flipped him over. He didn't want to look at it. He couldn't bear the thought of seeing whatever it was up close.

Click.

A small sound.

Click.

There it was again.

Sam struggled, kicking wildly, but his arms were pinned to the ground. There was no way to fight anymore. He'd have to look sooner or later, have to watch as the thing ripped off his head.

Beep.

He lifted his eyelids. They were heavy as though they'd been stuck together with glue. The sliver of moon spilled light into the clearing, and when he opened his eyes, he saw the monster that had caught him, saw what was on top of him. It was … it was … it was … *not a monster* …

Sam's muscles went limp. He almost passed out. He felt his eyeballs sliding to the back of his skull. It was only the laughter that kept him conscious.

Who was laughing?

Sam immediately recognized the hyena laugh. There was no mistaking — it was Javon! And there was someone else. Cody was laughing, too, and taking pictures. And videoing. That clicking sound. Those beeps.

Cody laughed. "What a scrub! This was the best!"

"Insane!" Javon cackled, pulling the mock turtleneck sweater down and revealing his head. "The best stunt ever!"

Sam watched them as though only half awake. It was starting to sink in. It had been a stunt. Everything. Right from the very beginning. They had tricked him. The accident — it was all a lie. That was why there had been no news report. That was why the cops hadn't come looking for them. Javon wasn't dead. He hadn't even been hurt. He and Cody had planned the whole thing right from the start. They had set him up. They weren't his friends. They had played him for a fool.

But ... how did they do the blood? That was real. Sam glanced at his clothes — no blood, just mud. *Impossible! That blood was real! I tasted it! It was real!*

Sam's heart still pounded, but this time with humiliation rather than fear. He shoved Javon off him and sat up.

"I got a great vlog of you, Maestro!" Cody howled. "You should see the look on your face! You're gonna be famous, man. Famous!"

Sam stood. That was all they had wanted — another stupid stunt to post on Cody's blog. Why hadn't he listened to his father? Why hadn't he listened to Mike?

He thought about fighting them, but he knew that wouldn't do any good. He thought of a million vicious things he could say, but what would that really accomplish? He could try to grab hold of Cody's phone and smash it to bits, but how would that make a difference to his humiliation? Besides, Cody had probably already sent the pictures and video off into cyberspace, anyway.

No, Sam wouldn't do any of those things. Instead, he decided to leave them there, laughing and slapping each other silly and making fun of him. He would simply step back and walk away.

CHAPTER TWENTY-SEVEN

All seven houses in Sleepy Hollow were dark except one. Number four lay straight ahead, and Sam walked with steady strides toward it. There was one final thing he had to do — one last showdown.

Before Sam could dig out his key, the front door swung open and his mother rushed toward him. Sam could tell by the redness in her eyes that she'd been crying. She threw her arms around him, taking no notice of the ragged state he was in.

"Oh, Sam!" she sobbed, squeezing him. Her tone was a perfect balance of relief and reproach. "How could you take off like that? Haven't your father and I taught you anything? Do you know what could have happened to you? Don't you have any idea?"

A smile grazed Sam's lips. *Yeah, I know.*

"I've been worried sick about you!" She pulled back and ran a hand through his hair. Then she hugged him again even tighter, pressing her cheek into his. "Don't ever do that again," she whispered in his ear. "Not ever — you hear?" Her voice quavered, and Sam knew she had begun to cry.

"I promise, Mom." It was a sincere response, since he had no intention of ever reliving the experiences of this evening again.

Miranda stepped into the doorway. She, too, had been crying. Now she smiled weakly and reached out to hug him. He rolled his eyes but let her do it just the same.

"Where's Dad?" Sam asked as the three stepped inside the house. His eyes scanned the hallway, the stairs, and the living room. No sign of Mr. Perfect.

Sam's mother and Miranda exchanged an odd glance.

"He's upstairs, Sam," his mother said softly. "In your room. He's been waiting there for you."

He took a deep breath. "I have to face him."

His mother nodded and let him go.

Sam climbed the steps as though he were headed for a hangman's noose. His legs felt like anchors, and the old wooden steps complained under his weight. The door to his bedroom was shut. He grasped the handle, and with a trembling hand, turned the knob and let the door glide open. A waft of cold air blew past him.

The room was dark, and the curtains were drawn. At first Sam thought his mother had been mistaken, that his father wasn't in there, after all. He was about to flick the light switch when he heard a fluttering sound. For a moment he thought he spied a figure stepping out from behind the curtains. Then he blinked, and it was gone.

"Come in," his father's voice said.

Sam stiffened. He searched the darkness. The words had come from the direction of his bed. He did his best to interpret the tone in his father's voice, but it was dry and flat, revealing few clues.

"Come closer."

Sam's eyes had adjusted enough to the darkness to make out his father's silhouette seated on the edge of his bed. He took a step into the room. It was like walking into a tomb. Sam shivered and watched the hall light catch a puff of air as it escaped his lips. He took another step toward his father, then stopped. The hall light reflecting in his father's eyes revealed the same blackness Sam had seen in them back on the Tenth Line.

"Why, Sam?" his father asked.

Why what? Sam thought while opting to remain silent.

"Why are you doing this to me?"

Sam said nothing. He feared what his father might do if he answered the wrong way.

Taking a deep breath, Robert sighed. "A guy makes a mistake, Sam, one stupid little mistake, and then he spends the rest of his life trying to make up for it. I did everything right. Everything. I never spoke out of turn.

I was honest, polite, kind, considerate. I held doors open for people, gave tons of money to charity, never drank or smoked or gambled. I tried to make up for it, really I did."

Sam was lost. What in the world was his father talking about? What mistake had Mr. Perfect made?

"Ah, but you wouldn't let me forget it, would you, Sam? You kept reminding me, pushing me, poking me. The Kronan — it was all you talked about. So tell me now. How did you know?"

What was he talking about? Sam searched for the right words, but his father continued almost as though he were talking to himself.

"It was that Barns boy, right? He told you, didn't he? And his father told him, I'll bet. Good ol' Big Mouth Barns. He could never keep a secret, could he?"

Nothing was making sense. Who was his father talking about? Cody's father? Had he known Cody's father? Had they been friends?

"I wish I'd never met that guy," his father continued. "Wish I'd never listened to him."

Sam's pulse quickened. He moved toward his father and sat on the bed beside him. Something inside told Sam to remain silent, but he spoke, anyway. His voice was soft and low. "What happened, Dad? What did you guys do?"

His father put an arm around his shoulder. It felt heavy. "It was a prank, Sam, just a stupid prank. We wanted to do some ghost riding, that was all. We never meant for anyone to get hurt … killed."

Killed? Sam's head began to spin. His father was a murderer? How was that possible?

"I should've known better. Norm tried to warn me …"

Norm? The principal?

"He told me George Barns was no good, but I didn't listen. I wanted to be part of the cool kids, so I tried to prove myself to them. We met at midnight …"

Sam wasn't sure he wanted to know what was coming next. And yet somehow he couldn't help but feel he already knew.

His father's grip on his shoulder tightened. "We took that bike — the Kronan — and we sent it down Vinegar Hill. George went first. He jumped off all right. Just sent that bike down and *whoosh!* It flew like a bird, glided forever. It took ages to get it and climb back up that hill. Then it was my turn …"

"But you didn't get off," Sam whispered. "You spread your arms. You closed your eyes and pretended you were flying. That's why you didn't see the car and the truck until it was too late …"

Sam stopped. He recalled sailing down the hill on the bike. He remembered seeing the vehicles collide, smelling the gas and oil, experiencing the whole bloody accident as if he'd been part of it. Sam had thought it had all been a hallucination, but it had really happened — just not to him.

"See now," Robert began again, his voice calm.

But the hall light glinted in his father's eyes, and Sam didn't like what he glimpsed.

"You couldn't possibly know that now, could you, Sam? No one knew that. Not even George Barns, because I never told anyone that. I told them my pants had gotten stuck in the chain. Only I knew what really happened. So how could you possibly have found out?"

His father's grip was tightening again.

"Stop, Dad, you're hurting me."

"You couldn't have known," he mumbled. "No one knew but me ..."

Sam tried to push his father away, but the hold was too tight. His collarbone ached. Tears of pain welled in his eyes. "Stop, Dad, stop!" he pleaded, his voice like a rusty hinge.

"You have no idea what my life's been like," his father said. "No idea what I've lived through, what I've done. Don't you get it? I didn't mean for those people to die. It was an accident. I'm sorry! Dear God, if I could only take it all back!"

Finally, with all his might, Sam dug his nails into his father's hands and pried them loose. Then he stood and moved away from the bed, rubbing his aching shoulders.

Robert got to his feet. For a second it looked as if he was going to lunge at Sam, who braced for the attack. Then, as though someone had flicked a switch, everything changed. Robert sank onto the bed, seemingly pressed down by the weight of his terrible actions.

"I'm sorry," he whispered. "I'm so very sorry for everything I did to you."

Sam was confused. His father was apologizing, but not to him. And as soon as the words left Robert's lips, something else occurred. The darkness lifted from his eyes. The blotches on his skin faded. He was transforming. In an instant he appeared normal again, the way he had been before they'd come to Sleepy Hollow.

His dad reached for him. "Sam," he sobbed, "I … I'm so sorry. I don't know what happened to me. I … I don't know. Sam, please, forgive me!"

Sam sat on the bed beside his father and hugged him. "It's okay, Dad. It's going to be okay."

"No, it will never be okay again."

Finally, Sam understood everything. Why his father had tried so hard to be so perfect. Why he had wanted him to be perfect, as well.

"It was an accident, Dad. Just an accident. It was a long time ago."

"It wasn't the accident, Sam. I walked away from those people like they were nothing. I washed that blood off my jeans like it was ordinary dirt. It was an accident, all right, but I should've stayed. I should've taken responsibility. I should've owned up to what I'd done. But instead I left, and it's been haunting me ever since."

Robert McLean stood and took off the scarf and heavy wool sweater. Sam noticed the room was no longer cold. "I know what I need to do now. I need to talk to the police. It's the only way to set this right."

CHAPTER TWENTY-EIGHT

A week later the sign was up and the real-estate agent had the key. All was settled: the McLeans would stay at a hotel in Toronto until they could find a new home there.

Sam accompanied his father to the police station and listened again to the horrible story of the stupid prank that had ended two people's lives. He watched the police officer take notes and tell his father they'd look into it. The officer said he wasn't even sure there would be any charges, given Sam's father's age at the time of the accident. His father seemed so relaxed, so at peace with himself, when it was all over. The curse had been lifted.

When Sam mentioned the prank Cody and Javon had played on him, the police officer was very interested. "Great! We've been trying to catch a couple of local thugs who have been jacking cars, taking them for joy-rides, and leaving them abandoned in fields and ditches. You've just provided us with a solid lead."

Sam was all smiles as they drove back to Sleepy Hollow to pick up his mother and sister and head out of town. They were leaving for good, and he couldn't have been happier.

The only thing Sam felt sorry about was that he was leaving AJ behind. When he'd seen her at school the last time, they'd talked. She told Sam she had no idea what Cody and Javon had been planning until it was all done. AJ had wanted to tell Sam that it was a stupid prank — even had a big fight with Cody about it. They'd broken up. She was the one who had put the note in Sam's locker. But the note had gotten ripped when Sam pulled out his binder, and AJ's signature and phone number were torn off.

"I don't get it," he said to her. "You knew about the prank from Cody's blog."

AJ shook her head. "I don't go on his blog, Sam. I think his stunts are stupid. I think his whole blog is stupid."

Sam couldn't believe it. "But … aren't you Homegirl?"

AJ wrinkled her nose. "Who?"

Sam sighed. He had been so sure Homegirl was AJ. Who else could it have been? AJ had put the note in his locker, but who had sent all those emails?

Anyway, it didn't matter. It was all over now. He was leaving Ringwood and AJ and Sleepy Hollow behind. She did give him her phone number and email address so they could stay in touch.

While everyone was loading up the car, Sam took a final look around Sleepy Hollow. He noticed the old woman rocking back and forth in her chair on the verandah, and suddenly he remembered something he wanted to ask her. Sam drifted toward the old porch. "Hey there," he began.

"What do you want?" she asked crustily.

"I was just wondering …"

"Spit it out, boy. Don't waste my time."

"I was just wondering … you said that lady, Hector, Heckly …"

"Hecate?"

"Yeah, that's it. You said she was coming back to Sleepy Hollow and that she's a witch."

The old woman grinned. "So? What's it to you?"

"Well, I was wondering which house she was coming back to."

"Why *her* house, of course. The house she's always lived in. The one she left empty a few years ago when she moved out west. Number five, of course."

Number five? Sam was confused. "But Maeve and Walter live at number five. Are they moving, too?"

"Who?" The old woman laughed as if Sam had told the funniest joke. "Maeve and Walter? You can't mean Maeve and Walter Moon?" The old woman chuckled. "You sure are one confused boy. Those people never lived at number five. They lived at number four, not five."

The woman was nuts. Really wacko. How could Walter live at number four when he, Sam, lived at number four? The woman was definitely senile.

"I think you're mistaken. I live at number four, not Walter."

"Of course you do — *now*." She peered directly at him as though she could see. "Walter lived there a long time ago. Before the accident."

"A long time ago? Accident?" Sam felt as if he were falling backward down a dark elevator shaft.

"Everyone knows all about that accident, but that goes back some thirty years. Tragic. Terrible. He and that mother of his were driving to see a sick friend. Bringing 'em lasagna, I think. They were cut off the road, and the car flipped. They both died. Some say the kid lost his head in the accident. Ripped clear off his body."

Sam felt woozy. He struggled to comprehend what the woman was saying. Impossible. It couldn't be.

"Yup. Number four. Those two lived at number four, all right ... and some say *they still do* ..."

She winked, and Sam nearly dropped to the ground. He steadied himself and glanced at his bedroom window. For a split second he thought he saw the curtain flutter.

The Volvo station wagon left the tunnel of trees for the last time. Sam didn't dare look back. Instead, he powered up his cellphone.

"Hey," Sam said.

"Hey," Mike replied.

After Sam told Mike the entire story and apologized for being such an idiot, Mike had forgiven him. And what was more, Mike believed him — or at least pretended to. Funny thing was, Mike was the one who had received the video by accident but had had no idea what it was supposed to be about. Mike was below Maniac on Sam's email address list.

"Check this out," Mike said. "I was telling my granddad all about your ghost-riding stunt, and you know what?"

"What?"

"He said that crap is so old. Said that some punks pulled those stunts even way back when he was a kid."

"You're kidding?"

"No way. He said only difference was they didn't call it ghost riding back then."

"Really? What did they call it?"

"Stupid."

Sam could almost hear Mike crack a smile.

As the black Volvo rolled out of the tunnel and away from Sleepy Hollow, bright sunlight beamed through the car windows. Sam took a deep breath. It was over. They were leaving for good. The station wagon turned right and began cruising down the Tenth Line one last time. Sam gazed out the window and watched as the lazy landscape drifted past. In the distance ahead he saw the blue Mustang approach. It zipped past them as if they were standing still. Sam glanced back over his shoulder. He caught a glimpse of the driver for the first time. It was Ms. Wolfe, his English teacher!

Cate Wolfe. Cate ... *Hecate?*

Her licence plate read: HOMEGIRL.

A shiver jolted up Sam's spine, and in that very instant his father turned on the radio. Loud bass hammered against the windows, and a hollow voice sliced through the dreamy solitude:

Ghost ride ...
Ghost ride ...
Ghost ride ...

MORE GREAT FICTION FOR YOUNG PEOPLE

WATCHER
by Valerie Sherrard

978-1-55488-431-5 / $12.99

Sixteen-year-old Porter Delancy has his future figured out, but his nice, neat plans are shaken when a man he believes may be his father suddenly appears in his Toronto neighbourhood. Porter knows that he wants nothing to do with the deadbeat dad who abandoned him and his sister twelve years earlier, but curiosity causes him to re-examine the past.

GIRL ON THE OTHER SIDE
by Deborah Kerbel

978-1-55488-443-8 / $12.99

Tabby Freeman and Lora Froggett go to the same school, but they live in totally opposite worlds. Tabby is rich, pretty, and the most popular girl in her class, while Lora is smart, timid, and the constant target of bullies. Despite their differences, Tabby and Lora both harbour dark secrets and a lot of pain. When the dust finally settles and all their secrets are forced into the light, will the girls be saved ... or destroyed?

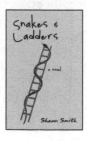

SNAKES & LADDERS
by Shaun Smith

978-1-55002-840-9 / $12.99

Thirteen-year-old Paige Morrow becomes concerned when the farmer who owns the property her family cottage is on hires a creepy arborist — a "tree doctor," Paige's mother calls him. When Paige befriends the arborist's troubled teenage daughter, Janine, and a group of rowdy locals, she's pulled into a maze of dark secrets and shocking truths that leads to a life-and-death confrontation.

Available at your favourite bookseller.

DUNDURN
www.dundurn.com

Tell us your story! What did you think of this book?

Join the conversation at
www.definingcanada.ca/tell-your-story
by telling us what you think.